The Quebec City Crisis

Roy MacGregor

An M&S Paperback Original from
McClelland & Stewart Inc.
The Canadian Publishers

For Eric Ruby and Brent Munro
– the original team

The author is grateful to Doug Gibson, who thought up this series, and to Alex Schultz, who pulls it off.

An M&S Paperback Original from
McClelland & Stewart Inc.

Canadian Cataloguing in Publication Data

MacGregor, Roy, 1948–
    The Quebec City crisis

(The Screech Owls series; 7)
An M&S paperback original.
ISBN 0-7710-5617-6

I. Title.   II. Series: MacGregor, Roy, 1948–   .
The Screech Owls series; 7.

PS8575.G84Q83 1998   jC813'.54   C98-930446-9
PZ7.M33Qu 1998

We acknowledge the financial support of the Government of Canada through the Book Publishing Industry Development Program for our publishing activities. We further acknowledge the support of the Canada Council for the Arts and the Ontario Arts Council for our publishing program.

Cover illustration by Gregory C. Banning
Typesetting by M&S, Toronto

Printed and bound in Canada

McClelland & Stewart Inc.
The Canadian Publishers
481 University Avenue
Toronto, Ontario
M5G 2E9

3 4 5   02 01 00 99 98

"*ICI!*"

"*Travis – une pour moi!*"

"*Moi, s'il vous plaît!*"

"*Moi!*"

It was cold enough to see their breath, yet Travis Lindsay was sweating as he stumbled and stuttered and tried to answer the shouts of the crowd gathered around him. How he wished he'd paid more attention in French class. If only they'd speak slower. If only he were standing closer to Sarah Cuthbertson, who was in French immersion, and who was yakking away happily as she signed her name, again and again and again.

Travis was helpless. He could do nothing but nod and smile and sign his name to the hockey cards they kept shoving into his hand.

He wished he understood better. He did not, however, wish that any of this would stop. As far as he was concerned – as far as any of the Screech Owls was concerned – this moment could go on forever.

"*Travis! Ici!*"

"*Moi!*"

This was what he had dreamed about all those long winter evenings when he'd sat at the kitchen table practising his signature. This was why he'd worked on that fancy, swirling loop on the *L* of "Lindsay," very carefully putting "#7" inside the loop to indicate his sweater number, just like the real NHLers did. He knew that his mother and father had been smiling to each other as they watched him work on signing his name, and he wished they could see him now. Travis Lindsay – Number 7, with a loop – signing autograph after autograph outside the renowned Quebec Colisée.

There was no end to the surprises on this trip to Quebec City. The Owls had come for the special fortieth anniversary of the Quebec International Peewee Tournament, the biggest and most special peewee hockey tournament on Earth. The Screech Owls were just one of nearly 150 teams entered, and Travis just one of 2,500 players, but every single player felt as if the Quebec Peewee could be *his* or *her* tournament, the moment where he or she would make their mark and be noted by all who saw them play.

Like everyone else here, Travis knew the history of the Quebec Peewee. He knew that it was here that Guy Lafleur and Wayne Gretzky and Mario Lemieux had all come to national attention.

More than fourteen thousand fans showed up in the Colisée to cheer the great Lafleur the night he scored seven goals in a single game. The following day, they sewed seven velvet pucks onto his sweater and his photograph was splashed across the country's sports pages — a national superstar at the age of twelve!

Wayne Gretzky's team had come here from Brantford two years after Gretzky scored an amazing 378 goals in a single season. Mario Lemieux had first demonstrated his amazing puck-handling here. Brett Hull, Steve Yzerman, Denis Savard, Pat LaFontaine, they had all starred here. And so had a young peewee goaltender named Patrick Roy, who was stopping pucks with a strange new style they were calling "the butterfly."

In the forty-year history of the Quebec City tournament, nearly five hundred of the young players who had come here had gone on to NHL careers — a record unmatched by any other minor-hockey gathering in the entire world.

The time might even come when people would talk about this tournament as the one where young Travis Lindsay served notice that he was NHL-bound. They might say this was where Sarah Cuthbertson, captain of the Olympic gold-medal-winning Canadian women's hockey team, first came to national attention. Or that this was where the scouts first began talking about Wayne Nishikawa, the best defenceman in the entire National Hockey League. Travis or Sarah or Nish – or Jeremy, Jesse, Derek, Dmitri, Jennie, Lars, Simon, Andy, Fahd, Wilson, Liz – the Screech Owls were all here, each one with his or her own special dream for Quebec City.

They already had their own hockey cards. And their own fans. Just like in the NHL.

Sure, the autograph collectors were kids, almost all of them younger than the Owls themselves, but the cards were real. Upper Deck, the best card manufacturer there was, had contacted every team headed for the Quebec Peewee, and team managers, like Mr. Dillinger, had handed out forms for the players to fill out, telling how tall they were and how much they weighed, what position they played, and how many goals and assists they had last season. There was even a question about which NHL player they modelled their play after, and another about what they enjoyed off the ice. Upper Deck had also asked for action shots of each player, and Data's father had taken photos of all of them in turn: Travis stopping in a spray of snow, Sarah stickhandling the puck, Jeremy making a stretch glove save, Nish taking a slapper from the point.

As each team arrived in Quebec City, someone from Upper Deck had met them with a large box of hockey cards for their team manager to hand out. The players were overwhelmed. The cards were of the best stock, complete with a glossy photograph of each player on the front, and a head shot, showing just his or her face, on the back. Each player's statistics and personal information were printed in fine gold lettering, and the team captains — like Travis — skated over a small hologram of the tournament logo.

Upper Deck also distributed the cards — by the thousands, it seemed — among the young fans of Quebec City. The free cards almost caused a riot outside the Colisée, where some of the teams, including the Owls, were lucky enough to book their first practice. The young fans seemed to know what the cards might one day mean. If they somehow had a card signed by Guy Lafleur the night he scored his seven goals, or by Wayne Gretzky when he played here, what would it be worth today?

Everyone wanted the captains' signatures. Travis knew it was because the captains' cards had the beautiful hologram, and he was trapped by eager autograph-seekers as he tried to plough his way through to the team bus after practice.

"*Travis!*"

"*Moi!*"

"*Une carte seule, s'il vous plaît!*"

He felt like a fool, unable to speak to them properly. He signed, and muttered stupidly: "*Merci . . . Oui . . . Merci . . . Bonjour . . . Oui . . . Merci . .*" He knew they could tell he understood about as much French as a kindergarten student. Why couldn't he be like Sarah, who was talking as much as she was signing? Why couldn't he be like . . . like *Nish*, standing over there in a huge circle of young fans, signing his name as if he was greeting his adoring public outside Maple Leaf Gardens on a Saturday night.

Travis looked over, puzzled, as he signed another card. Why was his best friend drawing such a big crowd?

By the time he finally made it to the old school bus, and Mr. Dillinger had closed the door on the remaining fans who were still holding up cards and calling out their names, Travis was certain that they were calling out "*Nishikawa!*" far more than "*Lindsay!*" He decided to investigate.

Travis finally found Nish, last seat on the bus, flat on his back and holding his right wrist up as if he'd just been slashed.

"I've got writer's cramp, man," Nish moaned when he saw Travis. "Real bad – I don't know whether I can play or not."

"Very funny," Travis said. "Where's your card?"

Nish suddenly blinked, surprised. "You want my autograph?"

"I just want to see it."

Nish made a big thing out of checking his jacket pockets. There was nothing wrong with his wrist now. He patted and probed and seemed happy to come up empty.

6

"Sorry, pal — all out. Can't keep up with the public demand, it seems."

Lars turned to help. "I traded him for one," Lars said to Travis, reaching back with a card. "Here you go."

"Thanks," Travis said. He caught Lars's eye. There was a message in the look Lars was giving him. He wanted Travis to see something.

Travis returned to his seat and compared Nish's card with his own. Data's father had taken a wonderful shot of Nish firing the puck from the point, and the head shot on the back was fine, but those were the only similarities. Travis had listed his statistics from last year — 37 goals, 39 assists, 14 minutes in penalties — and had said he tries to play like NHL superstar Paul Kariya. He had added that he played baseball and soccer and lacrosse in the off-season and liked any movie with Jim Carrey in it. Nish's card had his statistics right — 14 goals, 53 assists, 42 minutes in penalties — but there truth came to an abrupt end.

Nish had said he'd already been scouted by the Toronto Maple Leafs and the Mighty Ducks of Anaheim.

He had said Brian Leetch, Norris Trophy winner as the NHL's best defenceman, played a lot like him — not that *he* tried to play like Brian Leetch.

He had said Paul Kariya was his cousin.

Nish had his eyes closed when Travis made his way back to the last seat. Travis slapped Nish's knee, causing the choirboy eyes to flutter open. Nish obviously knew what was coming.

"*You can't do this!*" Travis said, holding out Nish's card.

"Can't do what?" Nish asked, blinking innocently.

"*This!*" Travis almost shouted. "How can you say you've already been scouted?"

"Because I have. And you have, too, or don't you remember Lake Placid?"

Travis shook his head. "That was nothing. They weren't NHL scouts."

"They were scouts, weren't they? And everything ends up in the NHL eventually, doesn't it?"

"But they had nothing to do with the Leafs or the Ducks."

"Well, I like to think they did. Those are the teams I'd want to have scouting me, okay?"

"And what do you mean you're Paul Kariya's cousin?"

Nish shrugged. "Don't get your shorts in a knot. He's part Japanese, isn't he?"

"So?"

"So, what do you think 'Nishikawa' is? *French?*"

"And *that* makes you cousins?"

"Sort of."

" 'Sort of'? You can't say that."

"I just filled it out as a joke," Nish said. "How was I supposed to know what they were going to use those forms for? No one said anything about hockey cards that I remember."

"You can't lie like that," Travis insisted.

Nish took a deep breath, gathering his thoughts. "I just exaggerated, that's all. No one gets hurt by an exaggeration. Paul Kariya? He doesn't even know, and he won't know."

Travis stared out the window all the way back to the drop-off point where the Screech Owls were to meet the families they would be staying with for the tournament. Soon the bus began its slow, twisting climb up into the narrow streets of the Old City. They passed horse-drawn carriages, statues, old churches, and drew up to a hotel that looked more like a palace standing over the frozen river. Sarah and Jennie were at the windows taking pictures of it all, but Travis hardly even noticed.

What if Nish was right? What if there was no harm in a little exaggeration? Maybe Nish did just mean it as a joke and Travis was letting his job as captain spoil his sense of humour.

Or perhaps he was jealous that Nish's card was attracting so much attention.

2

TRAVIS WAS SECRETLY GLAD THEY WOULDN'T BE
staying in this fancy hotel. He had never been
inside a lobby quite so lovely as the one in the
Château Frontenac, but he also felt that to feel
comfortable here he'd need to be a member of
royalty, not the captain of a peewee hockey team.
It was too fancy, too special. Even the doorman
intimidated the Owls, shooing them away from
the entrance, where they had stopped to watch
the hotel guests come and go in everything from
stretch limousines to horse-drawn *calèches*.

The Owls gathered in a large ballroom with
two other teams. The players were all given pins
and a warm welcome by one of the organizers,
who told them they were very lucky this year,
because their time in Quebec City would overlap
with the Quebec Winter Carnival.

They then met their billets. Travis, Nish, and
Lars would all be guests of the Duponts, a family
in which the parents spoke no English at all, but
the children – Jean-Paul, a bantam player more
than a year older than the three Owls, and Nicole,
who was their age – were perfectly bilingual.

"You can call me J-P," Jean-Paul said as he shook Travis's hand.

"Thanks," Travis said.

"*Bienvenue à Québec, Travis,*" Nicole said to Travis, smiling and reaching out to shake his hand.

"*Merci,*" he said, and felt a fool. He could say nothing else. Partly it was his lack of French. Partly it was Nicole. She was slim and pretty, with dark, shiny hair that fell over one cheek and had to be tossed back every so often.

Nicole offered the same greeting to Nish, who blushed, and then to Lars, who bowed elegantly, causing Nicole to giggle.

"*Merci bien,*" said Lars in a near-perfect French accent. "*C'est une très belle ville, mademoiselle.*"

When Nicole had moved on, Nish and Travis pressed close to Lars.

"Where did you learn to speak French?" Nish hissed.

"I don't know," Lars answered, looking surprised at his friends' reaction. "School when I was still in Sweden, I guess. It's no big deal."

"How many languages do you speak, anyway?" Travis demanded.

Lars laughed. "I never counted. But let me see: Swedish, German, a little Danish, a little Norwegian, English, of course, a bit of French . . ."

"*Et-gay a-ay ife-lay,*" Nish said.

Lars looked at him, dumbfounded. "What's *that*?" he asked.

"Pig Latin," Nish said, triumphantly.

"What's it mean?"

"*Get a life!*" Nish almost shouted.

Travis couldn't stop giggling. He hadn't heard anyone use Pig Latin since grade school, but, if anyone would remember, it would be Nish.

Travis was still laughing when Mr. Dillinger took his arm and pulled him aside.

"Travis," Mr. Dillinger said in a quiet voice. "The organizers are asking some of the team captains to keep a short daily diary for one of the newspapers. Muck and I thought you might do a good job. What do you say?"

Travis didn't know what to say. A diary?

"In French?" Travis asked, feeling relief all of a sudden that his French was so weak.

"No," Mr. Dillinger said. "It's an English paper from Montreal. Look, the reporter who's putting the whole thing together is here. You meet with him, you can decide for yourself. Whatdya say?"

"Yeah," Travis said. "Sure."

But he didn't feel sure. He knew it was the responsible Screech Owls captain answering Mr. Dillinger, not Travis Lindsay, who had never even written a letter in his entire life.

"I'm Bart Lundrigan, Travis. *Great* to meet you."

Much to his surprise, Travis felt instantly at

ease with the reporter. Bart Lundrigan was young, and he had a shock of dark curly hair that danced down into his eyes. He was wearing jeans and looked more like a movie star than a reporter.

"I'm with the *Montreal Inquirer*, Travis. We're not a very big paper, but we're owned by one of the big chains, which means the stories I write could, conceivably, appear right across Canada.

"The idea is this: a half-dozen of the team captains — players like yourself — are going to record their impressions each day in one of these pocket diaries" — the reporter held up a small red booklet — "and that is going to give fans a real insight into what it's like to play in this tournament.

"I want to know about the games, but I also want you to talk about coming here to Quebec to play. You know, what it's like to play where Lafleur and Gretzky once played. What's it mean to you? What do you think about the city? The people? Your billets? What kinds of things you do at the Carnival? You get the idea."

"Yeah, kind of."

"Good. Are you game, then?"

Travis was still wary. "How much do I have to write?"

The reporter laughed. "Not much. A page a day, if you can. I'll drop around every now and then and read through whatever you've done. Deal?"

Travis couldn't resist the smile, couldn't avoid the hand reaching out to shake his.

"Deal," he said.

"Super," Bart Lundrigan said. "I was sure hoping I'd get you; the Owls are one of the favourites in the C division, did you know that?"

"No, I didn't."

"Well, that's what they're saying, anyway. Lot of excitement about this Wayne Nishikawa kid – Paul Kariya's cousin, eh?"

Travis swallowed hard. He didn't know what to say. Was the reporter suspicious about Nish, or was he only making small talk?

"Nish is a good defenceman," Travis said, avoiding the actual question.

The reporter nodded. He seemed satisfied.

They talked a while longer. The reporter explained how he'd split up the diaries so everyone was represented: the West, Quebec, the Maritimes, an American team.

They talked hockey as well. Bart Lundrigan's dream was to cover an NHL team, preferably the Montreal Canadiens. He was, he said, not much different from Travis himself: both of them dreaming of the NHL, one to play and one to report. They had lots in common, even if the reporter was a good ten years older than Travis.

"I think this is going to be a great, great experience for you," Lundrigan said.

"I do, too," said Travis.

Travis was surprised he said this. But it was true. Fifteen minutes earlier, he had been dreading the idea of keeping a diary for everyone to read. Now he was looking forward to it.

In a small way, he was going to be a reporter, too.

3

THE DUPONTS LIVED IN A LARGE BUNGALOW well out of the Old City, on a street running down toward the ice-covered St. Lawrence River. The snowbanks were higher in this part of the city, much higher, and most of the houses had temporary canvas-and-aluminum "garages" to keep the snow off the cars, but apart from this nothing seemed out of the ordinary to the three boys in the back seat of the Duponts' minivan. Travis had no idea what he had expected of his billets, but he was pleasantly surprised to walk into a home where he could smell cinnamon buns in the oven and "The Simpsons" had just come on the television.

The difference was that Bart Simpson was speaking French – "I thought Bart was supposed to be a dummy!" Nish joked – but other than that, they could just as easily have been in a home down the street in their own town. The Duponts had a yappy black mutt they called Puck, frozen burritos for the microwave, and fights over the TV remote control.

No one, however, had much interest in

watching TV, for beyond the downstairs patio doors lay the finest backyard skating rink Travis had ever seen. There were spotlights off both ends of the house and, under the eaves, stereo speakers wired back into the house. The snowbanks were higher even than the boards at the Colisée, but it was the ice that most impressed the boys, so smooth it seemed to have been spread with a knife, not flooded each night with a green garden hose.

"*Je suis un artiste de la glace – le plus grand de tout le Québec*," Monsieur Dupont told them as he showed off his rink. He was grinning from ear to ear, his chest puffing out the bulky parka he wore as they all stepped outside.

Travis turned to Nicole, who was rolling her eyes at her father's bragging.

"He says he's Quebec's greatest ice-making artist," said Nicole. "It's not even the best rink in the neighbourhood, for heaven's sake."

The three boys all laughed. Monsieur Dupont stood waiting, wondering what his daughter had said to make their visitors laugh. "*Quoi?*" he asked her, and Nicole quickly said something reassuring-sounding to her father. Travis thought they had a nice relationship, father and daughter. He assumed Nicole had just told her father a slight fib, but where was the harm in that? He might have been upset if she had repeated exactly what she had said about his rink.

There was a big difference, Travis thought, between holding back something that might be taken the wrong way and throwing something out that would for certain be taken the wrong way, like Nish and his "cousin," Paul Kariya.

"We'll skate after we eat," suggested Nicole.

Travis felt a slight tremor go up his back. He had hoped for a chance to show how well he skated. He skated much better than he talked.

They ate a wonderful meal, with fresh cinnamon buns for dessert. J-P and Nicole had a brief squabble about what music to skate to, and then they went down into the basement to get ready.

Travis was first out the patio doors, and stopped dead in his tracks when he saw what was awaiting him. The rink, it seemed, had become a painting, a frozen island of colour surrounded by the pitch black of night. The ice sparkled and shone; there was even a red line painted across the middle of the rink for centre ice!

He stepped out, glided on his left foot and pumped twice with his right, the little jump he always did when stepping onto fresh ice. He felt instantly at home. What a strange, wonderful country Canada was, he thought. People who can't even talk to each other have a game that does it for them. From coast to coast they skate and play hockey, from the time they learn to walk until they're older than Travis's own father.

Travis loved real ice. He loved the way his

skates dug a little bit deeper than they ever did on artificial ice. He loved how, on a sharp turn, ice chips sometimes flew; on an indoor rink there would only be a slight spray of snow. He liked the way air felt outdoors: fresh and sharp on his face, more *alive* than anywhere else.

Lars and Nish were also out now – Nish trying his fancy backwards skating around the nets at both ends, Lars just looping around slowly, taking it all in. He had a huge smile on his face.

J-P was on the ice, and instantly there was a new sound in the air: the sizzle of weight. J-P was just big enough to have a big-league sound to his cornering, and when he came out of the corners, chips and spray flew behind him. The perfectly smooth surface, Monsieur Dupont's magnificent creation, was being destroyed, but Travis knew it was with his blessing.

There was another sound on the ice. Quick, sharp – the sound of Dmitri skating, Travis thought, although Dmitri wasn't with them. He turned fast on his skates to move backwards so he could see. It was Nicole! She had on hockey skates, and she was whipping around so fast that Travis stumbled slightly as he shifted again to skate forward as she flew past. He hoped she hadn't seen him nearly trip.

They played a quick game of shinny: Anglos versus Francos. The two Duponts, with J-P's size and Nicole's speed, more than held their own against the three Owls – but then, Travis thought, this was their rink, they knew it as well as the inside of their house.

Travis had the puck behind his net. He looked up and knew at once why he loved backyard shinny. No one cares. No one yells. No one corrects. Everyone was out of position. Everyone was simply *playing*.

He began moving up ice just as J-P came in on him, the older boy skating fast to panic Travis. Travis saw Nish off to his right, waiting. He had only one play, *the back pass*. It was Travis's favourite move in street hockey, and even though he'd often tried it in practice, he'd never dared it in a real game. It was too risky, too much a hot-dog play. Muck hated it, and blew the whistle every time Travis tried it in practice.

But there were no whistles here. Travis moved to his left, then placed the puck on his backhand and whipped it, across ice, to Nish, who picked it up before J-P, whooping with surprise, was able to turn towards him. Nish instantly sent the puck back to Travis, who was free. He dug in deep, aware that J-P was chasing him. He could hear the growl of J-P's skates, gaining ice on him.

Nish was hammering the ice with his stick for a pass. Travis skated up to centre, faked the pass and laughed as Nicole fell for it, sliding on her knees between him and Nish, who was still tapping hard even though Travis was now home free. Travis ignored him, skated in on the empty net, and ripped a snapshot in off the crossbar.

"*C'est bon!*" J-P shouted as he caught up to Travis. "Nice shot, Travis."

Far behind, Nicole slapped her stick on the ice in acknowledgement. It had been a nice shot, and it had gone in exactly as Travis had hoped.

He felt something big brush past him. A shoulder knocked him slightly. It was Nish.

"Puck hog!" Nish hissed as he skated by. It was a whisper, but one that shouted with anger.

Travis smiled to himself. Of course: *Nish* had wanted to be the hero. He had wanted to roof the shot that won the admiration of the Duponts.

"*Let's whip!*" Nicole shouted.

Nicole and J-P were stabbing their sticks into the snow nearest the patio doors. Then they cleared the nets off the ice, stacking them together at the far end. Travis and Nish and Lars stabbed their sticks into the snow too.

Nicole skated up to Travis and took his hand in her mitten. She got Lars to hold on to Travis's other hand, and J-P then took Lars's free hand and reached for Nish.

Around and around they skated, with Nicole leading the way. At every turn she built up speed until, finally, she all but stopped at centre ice and, holding on tightly to Travis, spun the line around her in an ever-faster circle, Nish at the far end gliding with the force of the spin.

"*Now!*" Nicole shouted.

J-P let go on his sister's signal and Nish took off, flying.

"AAAAAAAAAYYYYYYYYYYYYYYEEEEEEEE!"

The force of the "whip" sent him barrelling down the ice towards the largest snowbank, where he hit head first – and stuck!

"HELLLLLLLPPPPPPPPPP!" came the muffled shout.

Laughing wildly, the other four raced to pull Nish free. His face was covered in snow, and Travis could tell he was on the verge of blowing up, but Nicole took off her mittens and, very gently, brushed the snow out of his eyes.

The snow on Nish's face was melting fast, and Travis knew why; his friend's cheeks were burning red. Not from anger. Not from embarrassment. From Nicole's touch.

Suddenly Travis understood why he had been called a puck hog. He knew Nish too well not to see he was smitten with Nicole.

But then it hit Travis that so, too, was he.

"*Travis's turn!*" Nish announced.

Travis was delighted to be next. They whipped him the same way, burying him to his shoulders, and Nicole also helped him with the snow, much to his delight.

Travis couldn't stop smiling.

I have something to write about, he thought.

4

"DEAR DIARY," TRAVIS WROTE. HE FELT SILLY. HE didn't love this stupid little red vinyl book, but he felt that was the way you had to begin.

Dear Diary,

The Screech Owls are here in Quebec City for the most exciting tournament of our lives! We have already held one practice at the Colisée, which is the same rink where Wayne Gretzky and Mario Lemieux played when they were peewees just like us!

We were told the story of how Guy Lafleur scored seven goals and they sewed seven velvet pucks on to his sweater for the next game. I'd love that to happen to me!

Two neat things have already happened and we haven't even played a game yet. The first was the hockey cards made for us by Upper Deck. They are just like the real NHL cards. I must have signed fifty of them today. The next was getting to stay with the Dupont family and skate on their outdoor rink, which is the best one any of us have ever seen. We played shinny and then played "whip," which was a lot of fun.

Our billets, Mr. and Mrs. Dupont, don't speak English, but it doesn't seem to matter. Their children, Jean-Paul and Nicole, speak perfect English and translate everything for us.

Nicole played a little trick on her dad when she made a good joke in English about his rink and he didn't understand her. She then told him something completely different in French so his feelings wouldn't be hurt.

Lars Johanssen is on my team and he's billeted with Wayne Nishikawa and me at the Duponts. Lars is from Sweden but speaks pretty good French, which sure surprised Nish and me. (We call Wayne "Nish.")

Nish is more like me. He doesn't speak French at all. He made a great joke on Lars by telling him to "Get a life!" in Pig Latin, which Lars had never heard of. I think he thinks Nish is pretty smart and speaks a real foreign language like Pig Latin!

I did really poorly in French this year and don't think I'll be taking it again. I won't speak French to anyone — I guess because I'm too embarrassed — and I find it hard to understand when they speak to me. They talk way too fast. It sure is a lot easier when they speak English, like J-P and Nicole do for us.

I'm really excited about the first game against Halifax. We're supposed to be the favourites (or so they say), but Muck, our coach, says that Halifax is *the "sleeper" team in the tournament. That means that they're going to do much better than anyone expects. Anyone but Muck, that is, I guess.*

Your friend,
Travis Lindsay

The Halifax Hurricanes were indeed much better than most people expected. One shift into the game, and it was Halifax 1, Screech Owls 0, the "sleepers" jumping on a poor pass between Data and Nish when a diving Hurricane punched the puck ahead with his stick and the big Halifax centre picked it up and beat Jeremy in goal with a delayed backhand.

"*Wake up out there!*" Muck said when they skated back to the bench.

Muck was talking about more than the bad pass. The Owls had skated out on the ice to be greeted by more than six thousand fans. The noise had been incredible. Youngsters were hanging over the boards and waiting in the corridors for autographs. Nish – now known widely as "Paul Kariya's cousin" – was by far the most popular player, and Muck had to stop him from signing everyone's card during the warm-up.

The Halifax team had one superb line, and Sarah's line, with Travis on left and Dmitri on

25

right, was assigned to check them. Muck kept changing Sarah, Dmitri, and Travis on the fly to keep his match-ups the way he wanted, and it meant that Sarah's line couldn't concentrate on offence as much as they might have liked. Fortunately, little Simon Milliken got the Owls back in the game with a nifty backhander.

Sarah played brilliantly. She stayed with the big centre without letting up, and every time he got a pass she was there to intercept it or lift his stick just enough for him to miss the puck.

"You're getting under his skin," Muck whispered to Sarah as she came off for a rest. "Next shift, I want to see him go off."

Travis could see Sarah smile as Muck said this. He knew she got as big a kick out of checking players as she did out of scoring goals. Most players with Sarah's ability to skate and shoot thought of nothing else but scoring and being a hero, but Sarah was different.

The Halifax coach tried to sneak his big centre back out by changing the line immediately after the face-off. Muck slapped Sarah's shoulder pads and called for Jesse, who was closest to the bench, to get off the ice while Sarah leapt the boards and gave chase.

The Halifax centre picked up the puck at his own blueline. He hit his right winger and then burst up through centre, rapping his stick on the ice for the return feed, which came almost instantly. Sarah, however, was already there, deftly lifting the centre's stick as he looked for the pass, and using her skate to tip the sliding puck back behind him so she would have it free.

She was already past him, the puck hers. She took one quick stride and went hurtling, face first, towards the Halifax blueline, the referee's whistle screaming as she fell.

The big centre didn't even pretend to be innocent. He slammed his stick on the ice and skated angrily to the penalty box.

"Stay out there," Muck said when Sarah, still smiling, tried to come off. "Travis, Dmitri, Nish, Data."

The first power-play line hurried out, and though Sarah was still gasping for air, she took, and won, the face-off. She fired the puck back to Nish, who skated behind the Owls' net and waited. Travis skated past and pretended to pick up the puck, taking one of the forecheckers with him and leaving the puck for Dmitri, who was coming in from the other side.

Dmitri hit Sarah at the blueline, and Sarah tapped a little return pass between the defenceman's feet, leaving the puck alone for a moment until Dmitri, with his exceptional speed, caught up to it and started in, two on one, with Travis.

Dmitri would usually shoot in this situation – "You can never go wrong with a shot," Muck always said – but this time he came in and turned in a spinnerama, dishing off the puck to Travis as the defenceman played the body.

Travis was home free. A quick deke, a pause, and he snapped the puck high, his heart singing as it rang in off the crossbar.

Owls 2, Hurricanes 1.

After the Owls took the lead, the game was all Sarah's. She so frustrated the Halifax team, particularly their top player, they took penalty after penalty. The game ended 5–1 on a second goal by Travis, who merely tapped in a puck that Sarah left for him at the side of the crease as she drew the poor Halifax goaltender completely out of the net.

"Room service," she joked as they skated off.

"Thanks," said Travis.

"That one was too easy," Muck told them as they sagged in the dressing room. "Next one's going to be twice as hard for you, so don't get any fancy notions into your head."

He stood at the centre of the room, scowling at them, his eyes slowly moving over each and every player. Nish, as usual, had his head down, almost between his legs.

"Good game," Muck added, then walked out.

Outside, J-P and Nicole were waiting. Nicole hugged Travis, who'd been named Best Player of the Game for the Owls, even though he knew, and everyone else seemed to know, that Sarah Cuthbertson had been the best player by far.

"*Bon match, Travis!*" Nicole shouted. "*Très bon!*"

"*Merci*" was all Travis could say. All he could ever say.

"I scored, too," said Nish. He was practically between them.

"I know, I know," she said. "Nice goal, too."

Nish smiled, happy to be noticed.

"Who's number 9?" J-P asked.

"Sarah Cuthbertson," Travis answered. "She's good, eh?"

"She's *fantastique!*" J-P said. "*Incroyable!*"

"*Hey! Travis!*" a voice called from down the corridor.

Travis turned. The reporter, Bart Lundrigan was coming at him, his face one huge smile.

"Great, *great* game, Trav!" the reporter said.

"Thanks," said Travis.

"You bring the diary?" the reporter asked.

"Yeah, I did."

"Great! *Super!* Can I get it off you now?"

"Yeah . . . sure," Travis said. "It's in my bag."

"Great," the reporter said. "*Super!*"

5

THE SCREECH OWLS HAD A PRACTICE SCHEDULED for noon the following day at a small rink in Levis, the town directly across the St. Lawrence River from Quebec. Before they headed over on the old school bus, however, Mr. Dillinger and Muck took the Owls on a walking tour of the Old City.

They parked near the Quebec legislature, an imposing grey building that was almost dwarfed by, of all things, the largest snow fort any Owl had ever seen. The "fort" was actually the Ice Palace, where Bonhomme, the mascot of the Winter Carnival, lives during the festivities. Some of the Owls – including Nish, of course – got their pictures taken with the jolly mascot, who was kind of a cross between a snowman and a fur-trading *voyageur*, with his white costume topped by a long red tuque and with a red-and-blue sash around his middle. Then they set off in a large group. They walked through a stone gateway and down Rue Petit Champlain, which Muck claimed was the oldest street in all of North America. They toured a church that was more than three hundred and fifty years old and then twisted down so many narrow streets that eventually the Owls gave up trying to keep track of where they were.

Muck, oddly enough, always seemed to know. He would stand a moment, consider his options, then point in a certain direction, and always they would come out onto a main street where the *calèches* were clomping and jangling by, steam rising from the backs of the horses. There were crowds watching jugglers and clowns and men on enormous stilts. And everywhere there were young hockey players with team jackets or caps or tuques on – players from Canada and the United States and Sweden and Finland.

Muck led them behind the towering Château Frontenac and onto Dufferin Terrace, a massive boardwalk that had been shovelled off and sanded for walking. The boardwalk overlooked the St. Lawrence River, which was choked in a treacherous jumble of broken ice floes.

Muck pointed out a place in the distance where the Iroquois people had set up fishing camps hundreds, thousands, of years ago, long before anyone else came along to "discover" this land and claim it for any king or queen that lived in France or England.

"Right on!" shouted Jesse Highboy.

Muck told them where Samuel de Champlain had set up his first fur-trading post in 1603, and how the French explorers had all but starved to death the first couple of winters here. If it hadn't been for the natives, Muck said, they would never have made it.

With his big arms sweeping up and down the river, Muck showed them how the English ships had come down under cover of dark back in 1759. He walked them to the steep cliffs where the English had somehow climbed up from the river for a twenty-minute battle with the French that had decided Canada's future for the next 250 years, and was, according to Muck, still being fought by the politicians.

He told them that the old part of the city down below the Château had been virtually turned to dust by the English bombardment.

"Forty thousand cannon balls," said Muck. "Forty thousand cannon balls and ten thousand fire bombs – you think you could stop all that, Jeremy?" he said, turning to the young goalie.

Jeremy giggled. "No."

Muck took them out onto the Plains of Abraham, where Quebecers in rainbow-coloured outfits were cross-country skiing, and he showed them where the British invader, General James Wolfe, was shot and lay down to die in the grass as the battle raged around him, and then where the French general, Marquis de Montcalm, was hit by a musket bullet and lay mortally wounded.

"Did he die?" Fahd asked, breathlessly.

"That's what 'mortally wounded' means, son — but he didn't die here."

The Owls looked around, expecting a marker. "Where, then?" Andy asked.

Muck considered a moment. "The French carried their leader back into the Old City," the coach told them, "but the battle for Quebec was already lost. They took him to the Ursuline chapel, thinking he'd be safe in the care of the nuns, but he died there a couple of days later, and they buried him in the crypt. The British had already taken possession of the city."

"There's a *crypt* around here?" Data, the horror-movie buff, asked.

Muck smiled. "There are lots of crypts around here. That's where they used to bury people."

Data went silent, obviously disappointed.

"They kept his skull, though," Muck added, almost as an afterthought.

"*What?*" several Owls shouted at once.

Muck seemed shocked at such interest. "His skull," he repeated. "They dug Montcalm up about a hundred years later, and the Ursuline Sisters took his skull away. It's on display up in the Old City."

"You've *seen* it?" Data practically screamed.

"Sure," Muck said.

"*Can we?*" Andy pressed.

"You want to see an old skull?" Muck asked, pretending to be surprised.

"*Sure!*" the Owls shouted at once.

"Well, good," Muck said. "I didn't know this team had so many history buffs."

Travis giggled silently to himself. "History" had nothing to do with it. They just wanted to see a human skull, and if it had a hole in it where a bullet had gone through, so much the better!

"I'll make a deal with you," Muck said to Data.

"*Anything!*" Data screeched.

"You get a point the next match, we'll all go pay the Marquis a visit."

"*Alll righhhttt!*" the Owls shouted.

They headed back along a short cut that returned them to the Ice Palace and the parking area where Mr. Dillinger had left the bus.

Travis found himself dropping back.

"Muck?" Travis asked tentatively.

The big coach turned his eyes on his young captain.

"Yes?"

"Where'd you pick up all the history? That was neat."

Muck smiled. "There's more to life than hockey, Mr. Lindsay. Surely you know that by now."

"Yeah, but . . . well, how come you know all that stuff?"

"That 'stuff' is who we are. I'm a Canadian. I want to know what makes us the way we are."

"Oh," said Travis. "I see."

But he really didn't see at all.

6

SNOW WAS FALLING WHEN THEY CAME OUT OF practice at the Levis ice rink. Travis looked across the river, but he could no longer make out the towering Château. He turned his face upward, and the sky seemed neither to begin nor end, just to fade away into grey as millions of fat, fluffy snowflakes came drifting straight down upon him. Nish was also looking up, his mouth open as the large flakes landed, and melted instantly, on his cheeks and nose and outstretched tongue.

"*They're big enough to eat!*" he shouted.

Soon all the Owls were dancing around in the muffled silence of a heavy snowfall, their open mouths turned towards the sky. The snow gathering on the players' shoulders and tuques was fast changing the entire team from a variety of bright colours to the soft white of fresh snow. The Owls were vanishing before each other's eyes.

Mr. Dillinger was sitting in the driver's seat as the Owls boarded, but for once there were no high-fives or friendly shoulder punches. Mr. Dillinger had a newspaper spread over the steering wheel, and he was staring at it as if it were some broken piece of equipment he couldn't for the life of him figure out how to fix.

When Mr. Dillinger saw Muck approaching the bus, he folded up the paper and jumped down the steps, intercepting the coach before he could board. The two men hurried back towards the rink doors, where they huddled together under an overhang in the roof as Mr. Dillinger showed Muck something on the front page. Mr. Dillinger made his way back onto the bus, scanning the seats for someone in particular.

He caught Travis's eyes.

"Travis," Mr. Dillinger said in a very serious voice. "Could you come out here a moment?"

Travis got up, painfully aware that the other Owls were staring at him. There must be a problem, but what was so important that Travis had to be dragged off the bus for a conference with Muck and Mr. Dillinger?

Muck had finished reading whatever it was that Mr. Dillinger had showed him. His eyes looked partly sad, partly angry.

"You'd better have a look at this," Muck said, tapping a front-page headline.

Travis read the headline quickly, his heart beginning to pound: "PIG LATIN AS GOOD AS FRENCH, YOUNG ANGLO HOCKEY PLAYER SAYS."

Travis didn't understand. He read the byline: "By Bart Lundrigan, Staff Writer." He looked at the top of the page: *The Montreal Inquirer.*

"It's apparently run all over the country," Mr. Dillinger said. "I called home. It's in the Toronto papers. Vancouver. Calgary. They all picked it up."

Travis was still reading:

QUEBEC CITY – As far as some young anglophone hockey players at the Quebec International Peewee Tournament are concerned, the French language is no better than schoolyard "Pig Latin."

This is only one of many revelations to come from a series of young players' diary excerpts obtained by *The Inquirer*.

The "Two Solitudes" that first did bloody battle here back in 1759 are still going at it, it appears, nearly two and a half centuries after French and English forces met on the Plains of Abraham.

Take, for example, a diary excerpt from Travis Lindsay, a tousle-haired, sweet-smiling 12-year-old, who brags, "I won't speak French to anyone."

Lindsay, who admits to having studied French in school, shows nothing but disdain for Canada's other official language.

"They talk way too fast," he complains in his diary. "It's sure a lot easier when they speak English."

Young Lindsay compares this Canadian "foreign language" to the game of "Pig Latin" played in schoolyards, where children make up a silly language by slightly changing each English word.

Apparently members of Lindsay's team, the Screech Owls, have been making fun of French by choosing to speak Pig Latin instead.

Lindsay's billets, André and Giselle Dupont – who are putting Lindsay and two teammates up for free – speak only French. But talking with them directly is not worth the effort, according to the young peewee player, because the Dupont children "speak perfect English and translate everything for us."

Lindsay tells approvingly of how Nicole Dupont pours scorn on her unsuspecting father in English.

Another young peewee player, 13-year-old Brent Sutton, captain of the Camrose Wildcats, a team from Alberta, writes in his diary that he doesn't like the food and that, "There should be a law that all the signs are in English as well." . . .

Travis had read enough. He folded the paper and handed it back to Muck.

"Those your words?" Muck asked.

Travis didn't know what to say, he was in a state of shock. The words were kind of what he had written down, but he had never meant them to say what the paper was saying.

"I–I didn't say it that way."

Muck stared at his young captain, measuring him up.

"You got that diary with you?" Muck asked.

"Right here," said Travis, pulling it out of his pocket.

Muck read through Travis's first entry. He seemed satisfied with what he read. He didn't even bother to read the paragraph Travis had written last night before he went to bed.

"He's twisted everything," Muck said.

"That dirty son of a –!" said Mr. Dillinger through clenched teeth. "I'm sorry, Travis – I thought it would be pretty harmless. This is all my fault –"

Muck cut off Mr. Dillinger, who seemed near tears. "You want to keep on doing this?" he asked Travis.

"Not if it turns out like that," Travis said.

"Fine," Muck said. He stuffed the diary hard inside his jacket. "I'll be the one keeping the diary now, okay?"

7

BY MORNING THE SNOW HAD STOPPED. WHEN
Travis and Nish and Lars came up from their
bedroom in the Dupont's basement, they stopped
by the patio doors to see just how much had
fallen through the night.

Travis hadn't slept well. He kept going over
the contents of that awful newspaper article,
comparing it to his recollection of what he
had written in the diary. None of it seemed to
fit quite together. There were links, but all the
strings connecting them had ugly knots in them.

All Nish and Lars could talk about was the
snow. The world was whiter than any of them
had ever seen, the snow piled so high on every
surface, large and small – branches, fences, rooftops, telephone wires – that it seemed to have
been squeezed on, like thick layers of toothpaste.
Every now and then a pile on a branch would
topple over, the snow spraying into powder as it
fell, the sun dancing off the flakes and causing the
Owls to wince as they stared out.

Monsieur Dupont was already up and making

himself busy outside. At least Travis presumed it was Monsieur Dupont: a tall man covered head to foot, his face in a black ski mask that had two small slits for the eyes.

"*It's a bank robbery!*" Nish shouted.

"It's Mister Dupont," said Lars. "He's just clearing off the rink."

Sure enough, Monsieur Dupont was standing in front of a large red snowblower, brushed clean of snow. He yanked its starter cord once, twice, and instantly the silence of the morning was lost. The snowblower roared and coughed into action, and Monsieur Dupont adjusted the chute and put it in gear. The chains and tires caught and the machine jumped into action, the clear winter air between the boys and Monsieur Dupont filling once again with heavy snow. Only this time it was going up, not falling down.

The radio was on in the kitchen. It was in French, but the boys caught enough of the talk – "... *Travis Lindsay* ... *the Screech Owls* ... *Anglais* ..." – to know that the commentators were discussing the newspaper article Bart Lundrigan had written.

"You're in big trouble, my friend," Nish whispered as he poured himself a second bowl of Honey Nut Cheerios.

Travis snapped a quick look back at Nish, one that told him to sit on it and keep quiet. Travis didn't want to discuss the matter. J-P and Nicole were also in the kitchen now, and neither of them had said a word about the newspaper article.

The telephone rang. Travis thought he was going to hit the ceiling he jumped so high.

Madame Dupont answered. She spoke a few words of French and then turned to the table, looking first at Travis – hurt written all over her face – and then holding the receiver out towards Nicole.

"*Oui*," she answered. "*Oui* . . . Nicole Dupont . . . *oui, c'est vrai* . . . *non* . . . Yes, I speak English."

There was a long pause while Nicole listened. She turned to the table, twisting the telephone cord in her fingers and rolling her eyes to indicate boredom.

"No. He's already left for the rink," she said. "Sorry . . . Yes, I will . . . Fine . . . Yes . . . Yes, goodbye."

Nicole hung up the receiver and came back to the table. J-P and the three Owls were all staring at her, waiting.

"It was the local CBC," she said. "They wanted to talk to Travis about the article. I said you weren't here, okay?"

Travis felt immense relief. "Yeah," he said. "Thanks."

She had lied for him. No, fibbed for him. A white lie. A harmless lie. Instead of anyone getting hurt, Travis told himself, someone got saved: himself.

He knew that "Thanks" was not enough. The Duponts deserved more.

Travis cleared his throat. He felt awkward, embarrassed. "That article," he began.

"Don't even bother," Nicole said. "We know you didn't say those things."

Travis closed his eyes. Thank heavens; they believed him without him having to prove it.

"But I did *kind of* say those things," he said. It was spilling out of him. "Nish was kidding Lars in Pig Latin, but no one ever said it was the same thing as French. Nish just can't speak French either. And I said it was easier to speak English, because I'm so bad at French and so embarrassed that I don't speak it better."

"You shouldn't have written that thing about my father," Nicole said. Travis looked down, ashamed. But then she smiled; her point had been made and, as far as she was concerned, the matter was closed.

But Travis was near tears. "I know," he said. "I didn't know what that reporter was going to do with what I'd written. He took what I said and twisted it."

J-P looked up, grinning. "A better story for him, I guess."

"But it's not fair," said Nish.

Nicole smiled. "You get used to this stuff in Quebec," she said. "We just ignore it."

The side door opened with a waft of cold air that died the moment the door was slammed shut again. Monsieur Dupont was in the hallway. They could hear him stomping his boots and brushing the snow off his shoulders. They could hear him unzipping the heavy snowmobile suit he wore while working the snowblower. Travis noticed that the two Dupont children had stopped eating. They were waiting to see if their father already knew what had happened.

Monsieur Dupont came into the kitchen. His hair stood out all over at odd angles, uncombed since he had yanked off his ski mask. Travis could sense Nish was on the verge of a giggle, and knocked his knee against his leg to shut him up. There was a new tension in the air.

Monsieur Dupont came into the kitchen, stopped, and stared once, hard, at Travis. Travis swallowed uncomfortably. No one said a word.

Monsieur Dupont seemed sad rather than upset. He moved his mouth as if to speak, but then decided not to say anything. He moved instead to the sink, took a cup out of the cupboard above it, then turned to fill it from the coffeepot.

Nicole leaned over her cereal towards Travis, glancing meaningfully at her father and then back to Travis.

"I'll explain to him," she said. "Don't worry."

"Thanks," Travis smiled. But he was deeply worried all the same.

●

The team was to meet, again, at the parking area near the Ice Palace. From there, the team would travel, by bus, to the Colisée. Madame Dupont could drop the Owls and their equipment off on her way to her job at the provincial tourism office, just down the street from the Château. She seemed fine, smiling and laughing. But Travis noticed that when she got into the minivan the radio was on, and that she'd quickly turned it off before starting out.

There was a commotion around the school bus when they arrived at the parking lot. Nish was first to spot the activity out the minivan window.

"*Television cameras!*" he called, excitedly.

Travis felt a sinking feeling inside. No one would normally be interested in a peewee hockey team heading out for a tournament game.

"*There's more over here!*" said Lars from the front seat.

The Owls got out, and someone shouted, "*It's him!*"

Pandemonium struck as the boys tried to get their gear clear of Madame Dupont's vehicle.

Three or four television crews and several people with tape recorders and microphones with little station logos on them descended on Travis, Nish, and Lars as they sorted out their bags and sticks.

"Which one of you is Travis Lindsay?" shouted a hatless man with a hard helmet of sprayed hair.

"Not me!" said Nish, hustling to get out of the way with his equipment.

Travis was surrounded. He knew he looked frightened; he *was* frightened. The cameras were rolling. The reporters were all shouting at him.

"What do you think of French, Travis?"

"Parlez-vous français?"

"Can you explain what 'Pig Latin' is, please?"

"Are you having any trouble with the signs?"

"Do you think Quebec has the right to separate from Canada?"

"How do you get along with your billets, Mr. Lindsay?"

"How do you feel about playing a Quebec team today?"

The questions were flying at him, too many, too fast. Travis cringed against the back of the Duponts' minivan. Other reporters were at the driver's side of the van, trying to get a comment from Madame Dupont, who was hurriedly rolling up her window. She shook her head and put the vehicle in gear, forcing it through the throng. Travis watched as it slipped away from him until he was all alone in the centre of the parking lot, the camera operators and reporters circling him like wolves moving in for the kill.

"*Just a minute!*" a loud voice commanded. "*Un moment, s'il vous plaît!*"

It was Muck's voice. Muck speaking French — something Travis had never even imagined.

The circle broke as Muck barged his way through and took Travis by the elbow. Travis was almost overcome with relief. He felt like he had just been shaken awake from the worst nightmare of his life. He knew, even before it was over, that it was going to be all right. Because it was Muck.

"*Are you the coach?*"

"*Vous parlez français?*"

"*What do you have to say about your captain's anti-French remarks, sir?*"

Muck was already pulling Travis away from the throng. He paused, looked back, and caught the eye of the woman who had called out the last question.

"Just this . . . ," Muck said. The cameras and microphones instantly pressed closer. "There is no story here for you. Sorry to disappoint you — but there's no story."

"*How do you explain the diary entries then?*"

"You'd better ask Mr. Lundrigan about that," Muck said. "He's the one who made up the stories, is he not?"

The questions now came even faster.

"Are you accusing the reporter of making up quotes?"

"Travis — are you denying you said those things?"

"Why are you running from us?"

Muck had no more to say. He still had a firm hold on Travis's elbow and was half pulling, half leading him toward the bus. Travis wasn't sure his feet were even touching the ground, but he tried to hurry anyway. He could feel Muck's huge strength in his grip. His elbow hurt, but he wasn't about to say anything.

The reporters and cameras were following right behind, videotaping it all. But Muck never looked back. With Travis in tow, he rounded the bus and came to an abrupt stop on the far side by the door.

Mr. Dillinger was frantically at work with a rag and cleanser. He was wiping as hard as he could, but to little effect. Someone had spray-painted the side of the Screech Owls' bus. In large, crudely formed red letters was the message: "ANGLAIS PIGS GO HOME!"

Travis looked up at Muck, who had forgotten to let go of his elbow. The coach had shut his eyes, as if wishing everything would somehow go away. When he opened them again, he directed a helpless look at Mr. Dillinger, who was still wiping hard. But Mr. Dillinger shot back an equally helpless look: the paint wasn't coming off.

The reporters had seen it now. In near panic, they scrambled over each other to get their shots – some pushing and pulling, some yelling and shoving as they fought for position.

Travis felt, rather than heard, the breath go out of Muck.

"They got a story now," the coach said. "They've got their story now."

8

THERE WERE MORE CAMERAS WAITING AT THE Colisée. The bus pulled up and the rush was on, camera operators rushing and pushing and sliding and slipping and pulling and shouting as they hurried toward the bus, desperate to angle the shot so they would get both the team as it left the bus and the painted message on the vehicle's side.

Muck stood up in his seat at the front of the bus and turned to face his team.

"You walk out like you're here to play a hockey game, nothing else – understand!"

Each Owl murmured that he or she under-stood. No one – not even Nish – was making light of this.

"Don't talk to anyone. Don't even look at anyone. Collect your equipment, and go directly to the dressing room."

The players started moving. Travis felt as if he was going to throw up. There was a terrible pain in the pit of his stomach. He felt like crying.

"I'll walk with you."

Travis looked up. It was Sarah.

"Thanks," he said.

With Sarah by his side, Travis collected his equipment and sticks and began heading towards the door.

"*Voilà!*" a man outside called, pointing.

Sarah descended the steps first and turned to wait for Travis. He tried to concentrate on her smile instead of the cameras, and jumped down quickly to stand beside her. She fell in beside him, their shoulders touching as they pushed through the gathering horde.

"*Excusez*," Sarah said to one camera operator, smiling.

"*Pardon*," Sarah said to another as she began to push through.

"*Est-ce que vous pouvez reculer un peu, s'il vous plaît?*" Sarah said, very politely. "*Bonjour, madame, c'est une belle journée, n'est-ce pas?*"

Travis's first thought was that Sarah should shut up. Hadn't Muck told them not to talk? But then he realized what she was doing; what effect her French, and her lovely accent, were having on the media. They were moving. They were confused: if Travis was the anti-French Englishman, then who was this sweet French-speaking young woman who obviously cared for him?

"*Mademoiselle!*" one of them called. "*Une interview? C'est possible?*"

"*Non, merci*," Sarah responded with a lovely smile. "*Il faut que nous jouons le match du hockey maintenant – peut-être après le match.*"

Travis almost giggled. He wasn't exactly sure what Sarah was saying to them, but he was sure enough they had no idea what to make of her.

So much for the French-despising Screech Owls.

⬤

"*Stop!*" hissed Travis.

He and Sarah had just entered the corridor leading from the Colisée ice surface to the dressing room when Travis turned back and caught a glimpse of a familiar head of curly hair.

Bart Lundrigan, the reporter.

Lundrigan was standing in the seats. He was facing a camera set up on a tripod. Behind the camera were lights shining in his face. Another man was down on one knee, working the dials on a machine.

Travis and Sarah dropped their equipment and crept along the Zamboni exit closer to where Lundrigan was standing. The reporter seemed to be listening to someone who wasn't there, and then they noticed an earplug in his ear. He was nodding and smiling. He seemed very pleased with himself. Travis noted he now had a suit on, and a tie.

"That's correct, Peter," Lundrigan was saying. His speaking voice had changed. It seemed so practised now, so filled with confidence. "You wouldn't expect to find such incidents here at an event like this, but there you go. It tells us something about our country, does it not?"

"*Cut!*" the man working the machine called. "We just lost the line to Toronto."

Lundrigan turned, obviously annoyed. He was adjusting his earplug and fiddling with his hair when he caught Travis and Sarah out of the corner of his eye.

"*Travis!*" he called. "*Hey, wait there a minute!*"

The reporter yanked the earplug out and came running down the steps, two and three at a time. Travis and Sarah were trapped.

"*I'm so glad you're here!*" Lundrigan shouted as he hurried toward them. "*I've got to talk to you!*"

Travis didn't know how to respond. Sarah pulled his arm, but he stood his ground, still not willing to believe completely that this friendly, smiling man had done something so evil.

Lundrigan was smiling ear to ear. His *eyes* were smiling. He still looked like the nicest person Travis could have wanted to meet.

"You've seen the story?" the reporter asked.

"The coach showed it to me," Travis said. He did not return the smile.

"I'm far more upset than you could ever be," Lundrigan said. "Honest to God, I don't know what happened. What they ran was not the story I filed. They reworked it on the desk, I guess. That happens in our business, but they're supposed to clear any changes with us. They never called me."

"You mean you didn't write that?" Sarah asked, sceptical.

"Honestly, kids. I wrote a nice piece and included all the diary quotes. They took what they wanted, I guess, and made something wild out of it. I don't write the headlines, either."

"Can't you get them to fix it?" Travis asked. He felt relieved. He hadn't been wrong about Bart Lundrigan.

Lundrigan shrugged. He smiled sheepishly. "I can *try*," he said. "But I can't guarantee anything."

Another voice filled the corridor.

"Don't you think you owe this young man an apology?"

All three turned, surprised. It was Muck. He was walking toward Lundrigan, his hands down at his sides, but clenched tightly.

Travis could sense Lundrigan cringing. "I just did," Lundrigan said.

"I mean a *written* apology," Muck said. "Front page — same as your story."

"Who're you anyway?" the reporter asked.

"I'm the coach of this team, and I'm very upset with what you have done to this young man."

Lundrigan was almost like a puppy confronted by a large dog.

"I just explained a minute ago to the kids," he said. "It had nothing to do with me. They rejigged the piece and put that headline on it. I don't write the headlines."

"But you could write an apology," Muck said.

"I will," Lundrigan said. He was sweating, breathing hard. "I swear. But I can't guarantee they'll run it, okay?"

"You work for this paper but you wash your hands of what they do to your work?" Muck asked.

Again the sheepish grin: "Well, not usually – but sometimes they mess things up."

"You ever play hockey?" Muck asked.

Lundrigan blinked, unsure what this had to do with what they were discussing here.

"A bit," he answered finally, "but what's that got to do with it?"

"Travis makes a mistake," Muck said, "Sarah, here, doesn't blame him. Same if she makes a mistake. We take responsibility for each other on our team, mister."

"Yeah, well, that's all well and fine, but there's a big difference between a game and reporting –"

"*Is there, now?*" Muck asked. And with that he turned both Travis and Sarah around and marched them back to the dressing room.

9

TRAVIS HAD NEVER BELIEVED THERE WOULD come a time when he wished he wore another number. He had worn number 7 since his very first practice, when his father sent him out with a Detroit Red Wings sweater with the 7 sewn on the back and above it the name *Lindsay*. They were the same number and the same team sweater that his father's older cousin, "Terrible Ted" Lindsay, had worn back in the 1950s.

Now he'd take any other number – even one too large to fit into the loop at the end of the *L* in his autograph. Besides, no one was asking for his signature any more. They were still chasing "Paul Kariya's cousin," Nish, and there was huge interest in Sarah, who had played so brilliantly in the opening game, but the team captain of the Screech Owls, despite the magnificent hologram at the bottom of his card, was a bust. No one but the reporters wanted anything to do with him.

Well, that wasn't quite accurate. Most of the crowd seemed to know who was wearing number 7. There were a few boos during the warm-up, and shouts of "Shame!" from different sections in the stands.

"Pay no attention," Muck told him. "Remember, you're here to play hockey. It's what happens on the ice that counts."

The Owls were up against the other pre-tournament favourite in their division, the Beauport Nordiques. Beauport was just outside Quebec City, so the stands were packed with Beauport fans. The team also wore the *fleur-de-lys* pattern of the old NHL Quebec Nordiques, which apparently made for good television, because during the warm-up every camera that had been chasing Travis over the past few hours was down by the glass to get close-ups of Travis gliding past the opposition sweaters.

Nicole and J-P had explained it to Travis. The old Nordiques, with their sweaters so similar to the provincial flag, had come to symbolize the fight for an independent Quebec. Whenever the Nordiques played the Montreal Canadiens, the event was hailed and promoted as a rematch of the "Battle of Quebec," the same battle the French and English had fought on the Plains of Abraham back in 1759. And when the Nordiques won, it was a victory that reversed the outcome of the original battle. A victory for Quebec's independence, a victory for the French language and culture.

Travis couldn't follow all of this. But he got enough of an idea to see what was being played out here between the Beauport Nordiques and the Screech Owls. No wonder the cameras were here.

The Beauport team was big and fast and slick. Travis could tell from the warm-up that they were a superb hockey team. He knew Muck was concerned, too; why else would the Owls' coach have bribed them with a trip to see Montcalm's skull if they won? And Travis knew he would find it hard to play his best. He couldn't shut out the noise. The boos hurt him. And he had missed the crossbar every shot he had taken during warm-up.

Muck tried to change things around by starting Andy's line. He said it was to open up a bit of ice for Sarah and Dmitri and Travis by keeping them away from the Nordiques' top combination, but Travis knew it was to take him out of the picture. Muck didn't need the entire Colisée coming down on Travis's head just before the puck dropped.

The teams were well matched. The Nordiques were as good as Travis had guessed. They carried the puck well, but the Owls checked better, particularly Andy and Sarah, who were brilliant at centre. Jeremy was in goal again, Muck taking advantage of Jeremy's "hot hand," and Nish was his usual force on defence.

The moment Travis stepped on the ice for his first shift, there were more boos. He heard them as he chased a shot down the ice, and heard them, louder, when he first touched the puck. The first time he had the puck long enough to try a play – a simple give-and-go with Sarah – he stumbled and fell going for the return pass. The Colisée exploded with cheers.

Travis skated off almost in tears. He had blown the play. He had let the crowd get to him. He wished he never had to take another shift.

"You can answer them," Muck told him as he leaned over from behind, his big hand working the tense muscles in Travis's neck.

"H–how?" Travis asked. He knew his voice was breaking. He didn't even try to say more.

"You play your game. The people here know their hockey better than any crowd in Canada. You show them what you can do, they'll respect your abilities. And you don't have to say a word."

Travis tried to gather himself. He felt ashamed that he had ever thought he wouldn't want to wear the number of "Terrible Ted" Lindsay. By playing badly, he was not only letting his team down, he was letting his family down.

Next shift, Travis went in to forecheck, the boos seeming to chase him up and down the ice. He came in on the defence, faked going to one side and stuck his far leg out just as the defence passed cross-ice. The puck slammed into Travis's shin pad and bounced into the corner. He was on it instantly, the boos rising in waves around the rink. He stickhandled as the defender who had given up the puck came in on him, slipped the puck between the player's legs and danced out the far side of the corner with it, free for a play.

Nish was thundering in over the blueline. Travis hit Nish perfectly, tape to tape, and Nish wound up to shoot but, instead, faked the shot and passed off to Sarah, who one-timed the puck perfectly.

Owls 1, Nordiques 0.

"Think of the boos as cheers in another language," Muck said as he slapped Travis's shoulder and draped a towel around his neck.

The Nordiques tied the score in the second period on a splendid end-to-end rush by the same defenceman Travis had checked, and then went ahead 2–1 on a lucky shot from the corner that was supposed to be a pass but clipped in off the back of Nish's skate and in behind Jeremy.

Muck sent Sarah's line out with only two minutes left. The Owls were trailing by a goal, in a game they had to win, or at least tie, if they were to have any hope of reaching the finals – and, just as important, in Data's case, anyway, if they were going to get a look at a real skull.

They lined up for what might be the final face-off in the Owls' end, Travis up hard against the

Nordiques' right winger, who was determined to rush the net as soon as the puck dropped.

Their shoulders touched. They pushed. The Nordiques' winger slashed Travis quickly across the ankle. The referee either didn't see or didn't *want* to see. Travis looked up into the player's mask as their shoulders met again.

"*Maudit Anglais!*" the player said, spitting out the words.

Travis was confused. He couldn't ask for a translation. He knew he didn't need to. He couldn't pull out his diary and show the player where his words had been twisted by the newspaper reporter.

"You've got it all wrong," Travis said quickly. He looked again at the eyes. It was obvious the player did not understand what he had said. Travis cursed himself again for being so bad at French. Why can't I tell him? he thought. Why can't I even try?

He had to try.

"*Je . . . ,*" he began, tapping his Owls crest with his glove. "*J'aime vous . . .*"

The player blinked in what looked to Travis like shock, then laughed.

What did I say? Travis wondered, panicking. I just wanted to tell him that he had it all wrong, that I liked him. But it's not "*J'aime vous,*" for heaven's sake. It's "*Je t'aime . . .*" But wait a second, that's not it either. Oh no, oh no, oh no – I think I just told him, "I love you!"

Travis could feel the colour rising in his face. Mercifully, the puck dropped. Sarah took out her man and Data moved in quickly, plucking the puck free and taking it back behind his own net, where he quickly played it off the boards to Dmitri, on the far side.

Travis knew his play was to head for the middle. He broke hard, looking at Dmitri for the pass, only to find he was flying into the boards instead, crushed by the right winger's shoulder.

The arena was cheering wildly. They were singing, "*Na-na-na-na, na-na-na-na, hey, hey, hey, goo-ood bye . . .*"

The big Nordiques winger was leaning down, smiling at him. "*Je t'aime*," he said in a sarcastic, sing-songy voice.

Coming out of nowhere, Nish's glove hit the player's shoulder, spinning him around. But before the two could do anything, Sarah had taken a stranglehold on Nish and was wrestling him away.

It was the smart move. The referee's hand was up; the winger who had charged Travis was getting a penalty. And the Owls desperately needed the advantage. With a power play and less than two minutes left in the game, they still had a chance for the tie.

"You okay?" Muck called as Travis skated slowly to the bench, the boos following him all the way.

"I'm fine," Travis said. In fact, he could hardly catch his breath. His chest hurt. He had slammed hard into the boards.

"Good," said Muck. "You're right back out there."

Travis turned back towards the face-off, the boos growing louder still, as if someone had grabbed the volume control and cranked it as high as it would go. Travis had never heard such noise. And it was all because of him. If only it had been cheers instead.

Sarah won the face-off and sent the puck to Data, who fired it around the boards to Dmitri. Travis, grimacing with the pain, broke for the blueline and Dmitri hit him perfectly. Travis used the boards to chip the puck past the first defence-man, broke around him, and picked it up again just outside the Nordiques' zone.

There was one player back. Travis came in, ready to shoot, but then looked for Sarah, who was flying up over centre and had beaten her own check with her wonderful speed. Travis knew he had to try it. It had worked in practice. It had worked in the street. It had worked in the Duponts' backyard rink.

The back pass!

He knew what Muck thought of it. "This isn't

lacrosse, mister," he'd say in practice. But if ever the situation was perfect . . .

He could hear the boos, still just as loud. If he could pull this off, Travis thought, he might silence them.

Travis reached forward and put the blade of his stick in front of the puck. He had to be careful now; with the puck on his backhand he was working against the curve of the blade. He pulled the puck back until it was behind his skates and hidden from the defender.

Instead of bringing the puck ahead of him again on his forehand, he continued the backward sweep until his stick was directly behind him, the puck still on the wrong side of the curve, and he slipped a pass, backwards, to where Sarah was skating.

Sarah picked up the pass in full flight. The defender couldn't turn right, having already committed to Travis, and she blew past him, coming in on net and turning the goaltender inside out and down with two quick stickhandles and a shoulder fake.

She slipped the puck easily in on the backhand.

Tie game, 2–2. With the clock running out.

"No more back passes," Muck said as the Owls left the ice to a chorus of boos.

"It worked," Travis said, grinning.

"No more back passes," Muck repeated.

Travis said nothing. He was privately delighted with the back pass. But his heart sank as he turned the corner: the way to the Owls' dressing room was blocked by cameras and reporters.

"*Will you be issuing an apology?*" a woman shouted.

Travis said nothing.

"*We're told you will be making a statement — is that correct?*" a man called out.

Through the crush, Travis caught a glimpse of familiar curly hair. It was Bart Lundrigan, and he was being interviewed by another man. They were both seated and surrounded by lights and cameras. Lundrigan was talking, and the man interviewing him was nodding. Bart Lundrigan seemed to be enjoying himself.

Travis realized that the reporter had chosen the location and time of his interview very carefully. The Owls — Travis, Nish, Mr. Dillinger, Muck — were all a dramatic background for his television appearance.

"Inside," Muck said.

"*Mr. Lindsay!*" someone called.

"*Coach — can you give us a few minutes?*"

"*Travis!*"

And then they were through the door and had slammed it behind them, the warmth of the Owls' dressing room, the smiles of familiar faces, the cheers of his teammates, rising over Travis like a warm blanket at the end of a terrible nightmare.

10

MUCK WAS TRUE TO HIS WORD. THE SCREECH Owls had managed a tie, a single point, against the powerful Beauport Nordiques, and so they were off to see Montcalm's skull.

They parked at the Château Frontenac, and before continuing, Muck led the Owls inside and met with an older man who seemed to know him from a long time ago. They talked a while about old hockey games and then moved off to a corner. The man had a notebook and took down some of the things that Muck said. Most of the Owls investigated the hotel souvenir shop while they waited, but Travis couldn't fight his curiosity. He guessed that whatever it was that Muck and the man were discussing, it involved him. He thought at one point that he saw Muck hand the man a small book with a red vinyl cover. The diary?

Muck said nothing to Travis about the meeting. When Muck had finished, he and Mr. Dillinger paraded the Owls away from the hotel and turned into a series of older, smaller streets until they came to one called Donnacona, which was so narrow it looked more like a side alley than a real street. They came to small sign, "MUSÉE," and Muck turned in, with the rest of them following.

It was a small chapel. Apart from a few nuns, most of them old and all clad in the same grey habit, the Owls were the only visitors. Attached to the chapel was a small museum filled with period clothes and religious items, most of which meant nothing to the Owls. In a small room on the ground floor, however, there was a glass case on a desk against the far wall, and inside the case was what they had come to see.

Montcalm's skull.

"*Awesome*," said Data.

Travis would have used another word. *Repulsive*, perhaps, or *frightening*. There was nothing here that brought to mind the passions of the Battle of Quebec. There was no magnificent blue waistcoat or brilliantly white shirt, nothing heroic in the eyes as the Marquis lay mortally wounded, his men about to carry him off to the chapel where they hoped he might recover in time to save the city. There were not even eyes — only empty sockets.

There was nothing here to suggest anything but death, and the mystery of what becomes of you when the spark of life is gone. The skull seemed so small to Travis — too small, surely, to have ever been a man. He could not see the face of the Marquis in it, only bone yellowed with age, the grinning jaws containing just a few remaining stained and broken teeth.

"Can we take it out of the case?" Data asked.

"Don't be foolish," Muck said. "Show a little respect for the dead, if you don't mind."

Travis noted that Muck was practically whispering in reply to Data's near shout. Data saw everything from the point of view of someone who watches too much television. To him, the skull was a prop, just a toy. To Muck, the skull was the past, a real man who had suffered a real and painful death after a real battle.

Travis tried, desperately, to see Montcalm the man in the hollowed-out, yellow eye sockets. *What was the last thing he had seen?* he wondered. *Did he know that Wolfe had won? Did he know that his men were beaten and that he was going to die?*

Travis pictured the French general lying there, blood staining his white tunic and beautiful blue waistcoat. *If he had felt such pain just hitting the boards, how much pain had Montcalm felt? Was he frightened?*

He felt a current of air on his neck. Was it the heat coming out of a ceiling vent? The breath of someone behind him? Or Montcalm's presence?

He shook it off and turned his attention from the curious skull to the typewritten notes beneath it. There were two: one in French and one in English. He read the English.

It was a strange note. Instead of explaining the Marquis's life, it attacked the king of France for abandoning Montcalm in death. When the French and English settled their differences and put an end to their war in 1763, the king of France was given the chance to keep any piece of land he chose from the New World. Though the king knew his faithful general had given his life defending this land where Travis now stood, he passed on Quebec and selected, instead, three tiny Caribbean islands.

Whichever of the elderly nuns had typed this curious note, she had ended it with an even more curious line: "He let the Canadians down."

Travis shivered. *He did feel the Marquis's presence!*

Perhaps it wasn't Travis's fault, but that was just the way he felt, too – that he had somehow let Canadians down. *All* Canadians.

If only he'd never agreed to do that damned diary. If only he spoke better French. If only they hadn't booed . . .

11

"THAT'S MORE LIKE IT," SAID MUCK.

He was sitting up front in the Owls' old school bus as Mr. Dillinger made his morning rounds to pick up the players from their billets. Muck was holding *Le Soleil*, the Quebec City newspaper, on his lap, and Sarah, with another copy of the paper, was sitting in the seat across the aisle and translating a story into English for him.

Travis's original diary entry had been printed in full. The story in *Le Soleil*, written by the man Muck had met with at the Château the day before, was a scathing attack on the tactics of reporter Bart Lundrigan of the *Montreal Inquirer*. Lundrigan had been interviewed for the story and had come out looking very bad. He claimed that the quotes he had run in the paper were actually a combination of diary entries and interviews with the kids, but all of the players denied that they had been interviewed.

"He's been completely discredited," said Mr. Dillinger. "Serves him right."

"Why would he have done it?" Data asked.

"He wanted a good story," Muck said. "He

couldn't find one on his own, so he manufactured one."

"That's dishonest," said Wilson.

"There are good reporters and bad reporters," Muck said. "Just as there are good players and bad players." In other words, case closed.

The story in *Le Soleil* had an immediate effect that morning, and was first noted in the Dupont home where, at breakfast, Madame Dupont had greeted Travis with big kiss on both cheeks and a hug, much to his embarrassment. Monsieur Dupont was also pleased, and smacked Travis's back as he came for his second cup of coffee. Nicole and J-P had just smiled.

Nicole and J-P joined the bus with Travis, Nish, and Lars when Mr. Dillinger swung by the Duponts' house. The players were free until the game that night, the Owls' third, against a good team from Burlington, Vermont, and Mr. Dillinger was taking them all to the Ice Palace, where he would pick them all up later.

"*Ish-nay ee-fray!*" Nish shouted as they got off the bus. *Nish is free!*

"Cut it with the Pig Latin, if you don't mind," said Travis. "I'd just as soon never hear it again."

Nish giggled. "*O-nay oblem-pray, avis-Tray!*"

What's the use? Travis thought. Nish would never change.

Travis forgot about his problems and fell in with the running, shouting gang of Screech Owls and their new friends. He felt a mitten in his glove, and saw that Nicole had grabbed his hand. She was smiling.

"I have to stick close to you," she said. "Sarah says we're going to work together on your French!"

Great! thought Travis. If French classes were always like this, he'd soon be fluent!

They raced along the boardwalk to the top of the toboggan run, where they lined up to go down. Data waited at the bottom with his special wristwatch switched to run as a stopwatch. Nish was a good two seconds faster than anyone else.

"*Ish-Nay ampion-chay!*" he shouted in Travis's face. Travis didn't care. He was having fun. And Nicole's mitten was still in his hand.

Nish tried to buy one of the bright-red hollow plastic canes so many of the adults were carrying about – and drinking from – but no one would sell him one. It was still morning, yet some of them were stopping every few minutes and taking enormous swigs, the liquid splashing down their cheeks and off their chins as they laughed and yelled while at the same time trying to drink.

"I don't think it's Gatorade," said Nish.

"Neither do I," said Travis.

He finally found one sticking out of the snow beside a bench and carried it with him as if he were one of the grown-ups, but he threw it away after twisting off the cap and smelling the contents.

"Here, Trav," he said, handing the cane over to Travis. "Give this to your buddy, *Barf* Lundrigan – might help him write a little clearer."

They walked back towards the Château, Nicole pointing to everything, from the river to the benches, and having Travis repeat the French word for each. They then headed down the little side street where the artists worked, and Nish and Data and Wilson all posed for a caricature that showed them playing hockey, Nish with his stick broken and with his front teeth out and a big black eye as he sat in the penalty box.

They went down the side streets and stairs to Lower Town and the harbour area.

"Let's take the funicular back up when we're done," suggested Nicole. "It's only a dollar each."

Travis had never seen a funicular before. It was a sort of *outside* elevator enclosed in glass. It ran straight up the side of the cliff from Lower Town and stopped just outside the Château. Everyone agreed that it would be a terrific ride up.

After they had seen Lower Town, the Owls lined up for the funicular. It would take them all in three separate runs. Travis and Nicole, her mitten still securely in his hand, were in the first car, and everyone squeezed in tight for the doors to close and the climb to begin.

Travis and Nicole stood with their faces pressed to the glass. There was a jolt, and then the older part of the city began to fall away from them. They could soon see over the rooftops, and then all the way over to Levis. Up and up the cliff they went, higher and higher.

"I THINK I'M GONNA HURL!" shouted a voice from the back. Nish, of course, the fearless defenceman who couldn't stand heights.

"Bet you can't say that in Pig Latin," said Travis, and everyone laughed.

Travis felt so good about things. The article in *Le Soleil* that had changed everything. The backwards pass that had tied the game against Beauport. The little joke he had just made with Nish. The soft, warm mitten curled within his fingers.

The gears wound to a stop and, with a chug, the big doors opened at the top.

"*What the –!*"

It was Nish's voice again. He was at the back, and first off. There was alarm again in his voice – only this time he wasn't kidding.

Travis and Nicole pushed through to see what it was that Nish had seen.

There were cameras waiting!

Travis cringed, but then he saw that the cameras weren't pointed at him, for once. They were jostling for position around a wall to one side of the funicular.

The Owls all pushed out. There was a crowd gathered. People looked upset.

It took a minute for them to struggle far enough through the crowd to see what the cameras were filming. Then they wished they had gone as fast as possible in the opposite direction.

Someone had spray-painted the wall, in large, dripping, red letters.

"QUEBEC SUCKS! . . . FRENCH = PIG LATIN!"

"*Oh, no!*" said Nicole in a near whisper. Travis could feel her hand clench.

"*Regardez!*" shouted a man with a camera, backing away from the wall. "*C'est lui!*"

He was pointing straight at Travis. Others looked up and scrambled to move their cameras around. A reporter came running over.

"*You're Travis Lindsay, aren't you?*"

"*Leave him alone!*" Nicole shouted angrily. "*This has nothing to do with him!*"

"*Any idea who might have done this, then?*" a woman reporter asked.

Travis had none.

"*Get him out of here!*" J-P called to the rest of the Owls.

With Nish behind him, pushing, the Owls rushed Travis through the wall of cameras and reporters forming around him. Travis knew this would look like they were running away, but what else could they do? He didn't want to talk to them, and he had no answers anyway. He had no idea who might have done this.

Travis could feel that awful pain in the pit of his stomach coming back again.

12

THE ALARMING WORK AT THE TOP OF THE FUNIC-
ular was not the only display of hate graffiti. Nor
was it all anti-French. Freshly scrawled over bill-
boards and along the wooden walls around con-
struction sites, and even on the sides of the
Colisée, were the slogans "GO HOME ANGLAIS"
and "UGLY ENGLISH" and "MAUDIT ANGLAIS."
The New Battle of Quebec was being waged
with spray-paint cans, not muskets.

"Who can be doing this?" Travis kept asking as
the Owls gathered in their dressing room at the
Colisée for game three of the peewee tournament.

"It's probably lots of different people," said
Data. "Obviously at least two, because there's two
different points of view."

"What are they trying to prove?"

"*Prove?*" said Data. "I doubt they're trying to
prove anything. They're just spreading hate."

"What's the point?" Travis asked.

"To show that it's impossible for English and
French to get along, I guess."

"Why don't they come to the Duponts'?
They'd see we get along just fine."

Muck came into the dressing room, and all the players looked up. The coach looked concerned, but it wasn't about the spray-painting.

"I don't like doing this," he said when he was satisfied he had their attention, "but Mr. Dillinger has done some calculations. The tie with Beauport has put us in a tough position. We have to win by at least five goals tonight, according to Mr. Dillinger's mathematics, if we're to have any chance of making the finals. If we win, and Beauport wins tomorrow morning, it's going to make three teams tied at the top in points: us, the Beauport Nordiques, and a team we never even got to play – the Saskatoon Wheaties.

"Saskatoon's already finished their three games. They've got a tie, too, but altogether they've scored four more goals than we have and three more than Beauport. If we want to make sure we play in the final, we'd better win by five."

"We'll win by ten," Nish predicted.

Muck didn't even smile. "Five will be adequate, Nishikawa," he said, and abruptly left the room.

"Geez," said Nish. "What's got into him?"

"Nothing," said Travis. "He just doesn't like it when teams run up scores, that's all."

"*Ig-bay eal-day*," Nish said, shaking his head and bending down to tighten his skates.

The team from Burlington, Vermont, had yet to win a game – but they weren't that bad. They had size and they had heart. Travis had rarely seen a team work so hard. But as Muck always said, "You can't teach talent." And the Burlington Bears had precious little talent to spare, apart from a quick little centre and one defenceman who was every bit as good in both ends as Nish. Overall, the Owls were faster, smarter, and much better coached. If one of the two Bears' stars didn't do it for their team, it basically didn't get done.

Just before the opening face-off, Sarah had skated away from centre ice and, bending over, with her stick resting on her knees, had drifted by Travis for a quick, quiet consultation.

"It's up to us to get Muck's five," she said.

"We'll do it," Travis replied.

In fact, Sarah would do it by herself. Because he had to have the goals, Muck started double-shifting her towards the middle of the first period. She would take a shift with Travis and Dmitri, catch her breath while Andy's line was out, and then be thrown back out by Muck on a makeshift line with Derek Dillinger on one wing and little Simon Milliken on the other.

She played magnificently. Even though the Bears' coach was smart enough to have his good defenceman stay on her every time she was on the ice, Sarah could not be stopped. She scored twice in the first period and three times in the second – and with only five minutes to go in the game, and with the Owls leading 7–2, Nish pointed out something that Travis had been afraid to say out loud.

"*You can go for the record!*" Nish called down to Sarah from the defence end of the Owls' bench.

Sarah was bent over, gasping to catch her breath, and only nodded. She knew, just as Travis knew. She had five goals; young Guy Lafleur had scored seven the night before they sewed the velvet pucks onto his sweater.

"We're . . . already up . . . by five," she finally gasped.

"C'mon," Nish prodded. "Give it a shot!"

The Bears were giving up. If the defenceman or the little centre didn't carry the puck, no one else seemed to want it. They just wanted the clock to run out, and were dumping the puck from their own end, causing an endless series of icings.

Nish hated icing, and would do whatever he could to prevent one. Travis had rarely seen Nish skate *forward* as fast as he was flying backwards next shift to snare a dump-in before it crossed the icing line. He reached it just before the linesman could blow his whistle. The linesman waved off the icing, and Nish circled his net, still gathering speed.

Travis headed for centre. Nish fired the high, hard one – a play they rarely attempted – and it worked perfectly. Travis caught the puck in his glove, and simply let it drop down onto his stick as he crossed centre. *What a perfect pass!*

Travis was in with only the Bears' good defenceman back, and Sarah was moving up fast. He was on the left side, with a shot at a bad angle, but Sarah might be able to get the rebound. He didn't think he could get around the defenceman going one on one.

But there was still the back pass! Sarah was uncovered – the rest of the Bears not even bothering to come back with the game so clearly lost – and she was dead centre, just at the blueline and headed for the slot.

Travis slipped the puck onto his backhand, checked once on Sarah, and then pulled the puck back and around.

As soon as he let the pass go, he knew he'd blown it. The defenceman had read the play perfectly and, with the game already out of reach, had decided to gamble. He leapt past Travis, giving him a clear run to the net, but since Travis had already committed himself to the high-risk pass, he was doomed.

The defenceman picked up the puck in full stride. Travis was off-balance and turned, badly, into the boards. Sarah had been going full-speed towards the Bears' net and couldn't turn in time. Dmitri was on the far side, racing for a rebound, and he, too, was out of the play.

The defenceman was at the red line when the little centre turned and broke for the Owls' blue-line, directly between Nish and Data, who were backpedalling fast and trying to squeeze him off.

The defenceman's pass was perfect, a floater that the little centre knocked down with the shaft of his stick as he jumped through the opening between Nish and Data. Nish turned, flailing, willing to trip and take the penalty, but the little centre's skates were off the ice and Nish's desperate sweep met nothing but air.

The centre was in, alone, on Jennie. He faked once to his backhand, kept it on his forehand, and merely waited for Jennie to go down. Just before he lost the angle, he fired the puck high, ticking it in off the far post.

Owls 7, Bears 3.

Travis skated back to the bench with his head bowed. He could feel Muck's eyes boring right through his helmet, the heat of his coach's stare unbearable. He knew what Muck had said about the back pass. He knew he had blown it.

With neither coach nor captain saying a word, Travis made his way down the length of the bench and plunked himself down beside Jeremy Weathers, who was back-up goalie this game. Even Jeremy wouldn't look at him.

Travis sat, staring down between his legs, disgusted with himself. He felt a towel fall around his neck. Good old Mr. Dillinger. But then, he thought, the towel was also a sure sign he wouldn't be going back out.

"We have to have five," Muck said.

Travis could tell from the tone of Muck's voice that the coach didn't like saying this. More goals from the Owls at this stage of the game would look like they were just running up the score. Muck couldn't turn to the sparse crowd – none of them booing Travis this night – and explain to them why he had to have a five-goal victory. He just had to hope he got it, and could get out of this awkward game as fast as possible.

"Sarah," Muck said, "you're centring Dmitri and Lars."

Travis looked up. *Lars?* But Lars was a defenceman! He was being replaced by a defenceman?

Five Owls lined up for the face-off at centre. Sarah, Dmitri, Lars, Nish, and Data. Travis checked the clock. Less than three minutes to go. They *had* to have a goal.

Muck's hunch paid off almost immediately. Lars was so quick, so smart with the puck, he was able to pluck it out of the face-off scrum when Sarah got tied up with the little centre.

Lars circled at centre and dumped the puck back to Nish, who immediately tried his long floater play. He lifted the puck as high as he could, the puck flipping through the air as it rose over the Owls' blueline and centre ice.

The Bears' star defenceman had read the play correctly, and leapt to snare the puck with his glove, but it was just a touch too high for him. It clicked off a finger of his glove and fell behind him.

Sarah was already moving. She picked up the puck, moved over the Bears' blueline, and fired a quick slapshot that surprised the Bears' goaltender, who completely whiffed on the glove save. The puck bulged the net, the red light came on, and the Owls' bench, Muck included, went wild.

Owls 8, Bears 3. The five-goal lead was back in place!

Muck sent Andy's line out to check the Bears, and when Andy's line tired, he put back the same five who had scored the big goal.

With less than fifteen seconds left, Lars, with his uncanny ability to knock pucks out of the air, caught a long pass at centre ice. He moved in fast, completely fooling the only defenceman back by moving with a great burst of speed to go to the side, and then slipping the puck back into the slot area, where he was able to dodge around the defenceman and go in clear.

It was one on one, Lars on the goaltender. He shifted. He faked. He stickhandled so fast the Bears' goaltender went down on his back, lying there helplessly. All Lars had to do was flick the puck over the goalie.

But he instead skated to the side of the net

and turned, looking behind him. The Bears' star defenceman was coming in fast, racing straight for Lars.

Lars waited until the final possible moment, then flipped a saucer pass over the stick of the defenceman and hit Sarah perfectly for a tap-in goal, the net as good as empty as the goaltender turned on his back and stared helplessly while Sarah scored her seventh goal of the game.

"*You did it!*" Nish shouted as he joined the pile-on. "*You tied the record!*"

"Lars shouldn't have done that," Sarah laughed. "That was embarrassing."

"*It doesn't matter!*" Nish shouted. "*You got your seventh – same as Lafleur!*"

Nish wasn't the only one who had noticed. Tournament organizers rushed from the stands to congratulate her. The Bears, led by the quick little centre and the good defenceman, lined up to shake her hand. Reporters and photographers were milling onto the ice to get shots of her holding seven pucks.

How nice, thought Travis. They're no longer chasing me.

He still felt foolish about the back pass, but then, if he hadn't blown it, Sarah wouldn't have had to score a sixth goal and would never have been on the ice with Lars, who gave her the seventh.

Travis dressed quietly. Apart from one sharp look from Muck, who shook all the players' hands, nothing more was said about the messed-up glory play. There was no need.

When they left the rink, a light snow was beginning to fall. Nothing had been painted on the bus this time, Travis noted with some gratitude. Perhaps the whole thing was just going to fade away.

"*Travis!*" someone called.

He turned, nervous, instantly on guard – but this was no reporter. It was a young voice, though in the dark of the parking lot and the light snowfall, Travis couldn't quite make out its source.

"*Travis!*" called a couple of voices this time, and three figures came racing up, puffing and wiping melting snow from their eyes.

They were kids, all younger than Travis.

"*S'il vous plaît!*"

They were holding out hockey cards. Travis Lindsay hockey cards. They wanted his autograph.

Travis took the offered pen and the cards. He signed each one carefully, a big loop on the *L*, and the number 7 inside each loop.

"*Merci*," he said as he handed each one back. "*Merci*."

Travis's world felt right again.

13

THE OWLS HAD SIGNED AUTOGRAPHS AFTER THE
big win against the Bears – Nish still the biggest
draw – and then boarded the school bus. Instead
of delivering them to the usual pick-up spot
where they would meet their billets, Mr. Dillinger
took them out on the main road towards the university, where they turned down the Duponts'
street and parked opposite their driveway, where
Nicole and J-P and several of their friends from
the neighbourhood were waiting.

"Now you skate for fun!" Mr. Dillinger announced as he turned off the engine and yanked
on the emergency brake.

It was a wonderful surprise, arranged almost
entirely by Nicole and J-P. Monsieur Dupont
was just putting away the snowblower. The ice
glistened, the perfect result of a careful flood.
There were patio lanterns strung on poles
around the rink. Madame Dupont had hot
chocolate for everyone, and homemade cookies
and tarts and tiny chocolate *bonbons* that she had
made herself.

The Owls all had their skates. They put them on while sitting on benches in the tent garage, then stepped carefully along a path made by Monsieur Dupont's snowblower, then onto the ice. J-P had set up the sound system so it would first play a song in English that everyone knew, then a French song, then an English song again. All the Quebec kids knew the French songs by heart, and the others, like Sarah and Travis, wondered why they had never heard them before, for the music was wonderful.

They skated in circles to the music. They played "whip" until Nish was so exhausted he lay on his back like a beached whale on top of the far snowbank, tossing mittfuls of snow onto his own face, where it melted and cooled him. They drank hot chocolate and ate candies and regretted that soon Muck's curfew would be in force and Mr. Dillinger would have to deliver them all back to their billets.

"Let's go for a walk," Nicole said to Travis. "Sometimes from the end of the street you can see the northern lights."

They slipped away down the path, tiptoeing on their skates until they reached the tent garage, and then quickly changed into their boots.

Travis's feet always felt odd when he first put on his boots after skating, but particularly so after skating on an open-air rink. They felt slightly unsteady, like he had rubber bands connecting his joints instead of muscles.

He pretended to stumble and reached out and took Nicole's hand. She giggled softly. He could feel the colour rising in his face. He knew his move must have looked pretty dumb – faking a fall so he had to grab something to hold him up. But Nicole didn't seem to mind. She tightened her grip on Travis's hand. He felt his face turn even hotter.

They were away from the lights now. The street was dark but for a few streetlights. Travis looked up; the stars were thick and plentiful. He recognized Orion by the belt, the Big Dipper by its handle. He wondered if he should point them out to Nicole. She might be impressed. But he knew only two constellations. If she asked about any others, he wouldn't have a clue.

"There," she said. "You can see them rippling."

Travis knew Nicole was referring to the northern lights, but he wasn't looking up any more.

A dark shape was moving by the school bus!

Something was there, but he didn't know what. A big dog? A person? He had seen a shadow, and the shadow had jumped as if it was hiding.

"*Shhhhhhh,*" he said.

Nicole turned, surprised, and saw that Travis was pointing toward the bus. They ducked into the nearest driveway, using the high snowbanks as cover. They peeked out from behind, waiting.

"What's going on?" Nicole whispered.

"I don't know."

"Is it one of your team?"

"I don't think so."

They watched for a moment. It was definitely a person. Whoever it was, he was wearing a bulky parka, with the hood drawn up. The hood had a thick fringe of fur, so his face was hidden.

The figure rounded the side of the bus. A big glove came off, and a hand went into a side pocket and came out with a can of something.

"Spray-paint," whispered Nicole.

"What'll we do?"

"I'd better get my father!" Nicole said.

The two of them cut through the deep snow of a neighbour's backyard. They scrambled over the Dupont's back fence and ploughed through the heavy snow until, with difficulty, they climbed the snowbank at the far end of the rink, rising over it just as Nish, still lying on his back and eating snow, caught sight of them.

"*Ohhhhhhhh — where–have–you–two–been?*" Nish sang in his most irritating voice.

Nicole and Travis were bounding down the side of the snowbank.

"Where's Muck?" Travis called.

Nish pointed towards the patio doors.

Nicole was already at the back of the house. She yanked the patio doors open and ran in, her mother shouting at her – probably about getting snow all over the carpet, Travis figured.

By the time Travis got inside, Nicole was calling to her father, who was already up and moving.

"There's someone painting the bus!" Travis shouted at Muck and Mr. Dillinger, who had been sitting over a cup of coffee with Monsieur Dupont. There was a cribbage board and cards on the table and a hockey game on TV. Montreal Canadiens versus the Mighty Ducks of Anaheim, Travis noted. Strange, he'd been so caught up in this tournament, he'd almost forgotten about the NHL. He tried never to miss "Hockey Night in Canada" when Paul Kariya was on.

Muck was pulling on his big snow boots, reaching for his coat. Monsieur Dupont was already at the door. Mr. Dillinger was struggling to tuck in his shirt.

"Vite!" Monsieur Dupont called to his wife. *"La police!"*

Madame Dupont moved quickly towards the downstairs telephone.

Muck and Monsieur Dupont were out the door, doing up buttons and zippers as they ran.

Through the glass of the patio door, Travis could see the kids all standing on the ice, watching with puzzled faces. Everyone knew something was up.

Travis and Nicole fell in behind the men. As the only two already out of their skates, they were the only ones who could follow.

Travis had barely reached the end of the Duponts' driveway when he saw Muck in full flight down the street toward the bus.

The spray-painter in the hooded parka saw him and bolted. Whoever it was, he was very fast.

Muck turned and yelled at Monsieur Dupont, who had fallen in behind him.

"*La voiture!*" Muck shouted.

Monsieur Dupont spun on his heels and ran back to his car, started it up, and backed out with the heavy winter tires spinning a sudden spray of snow. He switched to a forward gear and sped away, the car fishtailing down the street as he joined in the chase.

"*C'mon!*" shouted Nicole. "*We can cut him off this way!*"

To Travis, they seemed to be running in the wrong direction. But Nicole knew how the streets ran. She and Travis dashed up one block, across another street, then turned right.

Down the street Travis could see the hooded spray-painter, running straight towards them. Muck was still in pursuit, but had fallen behind.

He was coming closer! Travis had no idea what to do.

What if he had a gun?

What if he had a knife?

"*We have to turn him!*" Nicole shouted.

There was just one side street between them and the hooded figure. She jumped in the air and shouted.

"*Yahhhhhhhh!*"

Travis didn't know what to do. He jumped up and shouted, too.

"*Yaaaahhhhhhhhhh!*"

He hoped their winter clothes made them look bigger than they were. It didn't matter, though, as Nicole was already racing towards the spray-painter. Travis joined her, praying that the dark figure would turn away from them into the side street.

He did!

His face still hidden deep inside his hood, he took one look up at Nicole and Travis, then one look back at Muck, who was grimly churning up the street towards him. Mr. Dillinger was now in view farther back, still trying to tuck in his shirt as he ran, jacketless, after the man who'd dared deface his bus.

Just as the hooded figure turned, a pair of extremely bright headlights snapped on, catching him in their harsh light and bringing him to a stop as suddenly as if he'd just run into a wall.

It was Monsieur Dupont. He had been lying in wait in his car, his headlights off.

That moment's hesitation was all Muck needed. He dropped his shoulder and charged straight at the spray-painter. The man's knees buckled, spilling him onto the road with Muck hanging on tight.

Monsieur Dupont shot the car forward, then jammed on the brakes, causing the car to slide halfway up a snowbank, where it hung helplessly, the snow frying in the heat of the exhaust system and steam rising from under the rear wheels.

Mr. Dillinger, his shirt flapping loose, went down on one knee, spinning into Muck and the hooded figure as they lay on the icy road. He grabbed the man by both shoulders and slammed him hard down on the ice.

A siren howled!

Travis and Nicole turned quickly to see where the awful sound was coming from. Three police cruisers, their lights flashing, were turning towards them off the Duponts' street, the cars swaying dangerously on the ice.

Monsieur Dupont roughly grabbed the can of spray-paint and tossed it angrily into the nearest snowbank.

Muck was up on his knees now. He seized the hood of the parka and yanked hard.

Travis gasped. He couldn't believe what he saw as the hood came down.

Brown, curly hair.

It was Bart Lundrigan – the reporter from the *Montreal Inquirer*.

14

"HE WASN'T CONTENT WITH JUST *REPORTING* the news — it seems he had to *create* it, too."

The man speaking was the editor of the *Montreal Inquirer*, a big man, with a face as round and red as a face-off circle. He had come up to Quebec City to meet with police and apologize to the people of Quebec City for all the trouble Bart Lundrigan had created.

He met separately with the Owls and those parents who had come along on the trip, and he both apologized profusely to the team and handed over a cheque for one thousand dollars to Mr. Dillinger, who said that it would go towards cleaning up the old school bus and that the remainder would be put into the local minor-hockey program once the Owls got back home.

The newspaper editor's explanation for his reporter's behaviour confirmed what everyone had guessed. Bart Lundrigan had simply been too ambitious. He dreamed of getting to the NHL as a reporter, and he must have figured that breaking a major story involving minor hockey would get him there faster.

The editor said that his newspaper hadn't changed a single word of Lundrigan's original story, despite the reporter's claim that this whole affair only got started when someone at the *Inquirer* meddled with his work.

Lundrigan must have figured that all the interviews he would get because of his sensational story were going to get him closer to his dream of a bigger and better job. And after the article in *Le Soleil* had thrown his reputation into doubt, he had taken matters into his own hands to prove he really did have a story. It had been Lundrigan who had spray-painted all those hate-filled messages over the city – both the anti-French and anti-English. There never were two warring sides. One man with a single can of spray-paint had created something that the rest of the media was treating as a huge crisis.

Lundrigan had been charged by the police with public mischief and with defacing public property. He had been fired by the *Inquirer*, and his career as a reporter was over, because he could no longer be trusted. He had made much more out of things than was really there, had taken something true and twisted it into a lie.

Among the many victims of Bart Lundrigan's lies were the people of Quebec City. They felt terrible about Travis Lindsay, the little peewee player who had borne the brunt of their anger.

Travis, once again, became the focus of the

media. But now the cameras seemed to be smiling at him. It was a strange experience, like landing on two different planets, and yet he had not changed. Just the way they saw him was different.

Travis was asked to go on a French television program called "Le Point" with Muck and Monsieur Dupont, but said he couldn't do it. The woman who had approached him with the idea put his refusal down to the nerves of a quiet-spoken, shy young boy. She hadn't asked if he spoke any French. Perhaps they had been planning to translate whatever he said. But Travis couldn't do it. He was ashamed that he hadn't the nerve even to try speaking French.

●

"*You* are coming with us," Nicole Dupont said, as she took Travis by the arm and pulled him away from the rest of the Owls. Travis was surprised by the sneak attack, but delighted that it was his new friend, Nicole. Right behind Nicole, also smiling, was Sarah Cuthbertson.

"Where are we going?" Travis giggled as Sarah took his other arm, marching him towards the door.

"School," she said. Nothing else.

15

"*ET LE NUMERO SEPT, NUMBER SEVEN, LE CAPI-
taine des Screech Owls, the Screech Owls' captain,
Traaaa-vis Liiiinnnnnnddddddd-say!*"

A moment ago, Travis had been standing at
the gate leading onto the Colisée ice. He had
been surrounded by black, the lights down low in
the packed arena. Now, as the Colisée announcer
called his number, and his name rumbled and
echoed about the building, spotlights and lasers
exploded from the rafters.

Travis skated out, but he had no sense of his
skates ever touching the ice. He felt as if he were
floating on air. His Screech Owls uniform shone
brilliantly under the spotlights, and those lights
and the roar of the crowd had tracked him all the
way to the blueline, where his skates somehow
managed on their own to bring him to a graceful
stop. He stood, unsteadily, beside Nish and Data
and Jenny and Jeremy, who had already been
introduced and were standing there waiting, skit-
tering back and forth on their skates.

Nish turned and slammed his stick into Travis's

shinpads. He had a big, wide smile on his face. He knew what was going on.

The rise continued to grow. It built and built from the moment Travis's name was announced until it seemed it would go on forever, the Colisée filling with the roar of thousands upon thousands of voices. It was a noise so utterly different from the fierce roar of the crowd the last time Travis and the Owls had played Beauport.

Travis turned on his skates. He looked down modestly at his laces. But still the roar built. They wouldn't quit. He looked toward the doorway. Sarah was standing there, waiting, a big smile on her face as she looked out at Travis, who was shifting more and more uncomfortably on the blueline, the roar holding fast, deafening.

Nish's stick slammed again into his shinpads. Travis could hear him shouting, only it was muffled, as if there were three walls between them, not three feet. He had to lean into Nish to make out what he was saying.

"Acknowledge them!" Nish was screaming. *"They're waiting for you to do something!"*

Travis, in his shyness, hadn't understood. Nish, of course, understood perfectly the rules and regulations of being the centre of attention.

Travis skated out in a small loop. He raised his stick like a sword and saluted the crowd.

The roar nearly split his eardrums! It built to an impossible pitch, then at last died suddenly away.

The fans sat, as one, back into their seats, and the announcer began to introduce Sarah, which caused the roaring to begin all over again.

Everyone knew about the girl who had tied Guy Lafleur's record of seven goals. It seemed that even the souvenir hunters knew about Sarah's great achievement, for as the team had dressed for the final game, Sarah was unable to find her Screech Owls sweater. Someone had taken her jersey with her lucky number. Mr. Dillinger had been forced to go to the equipment bag and find a replacement, and instead of wearing her usual number 9, Sarah now had to skate out with the number 28 on her back. She didn't seem too pleased about it.

Sarah saluted the crowd, and then, one by one, the rest of the Owls came out to loud applause and cheers: Dmitri, Simon, Jesse, Lars . . .

The Owls assembled on the blueline until the coach, Muck Munro, was introduced and the roar exploded one more time. Muck gave an embarrassed little wave as he walked, unsteadily, around the boards towards the Owls' bench.

After the Owls had all been introduced, the announcer turned to the Beauport Nordiques, the other team to reach the championship game in the Quebec International Peewee Tournament. The Saskatoon Wheaties, despite the same overall record, had been eliminated from the final because they hadn't scored as many goals as the other two teams. The significance of Sarah's seven goals was now known to everyone and appreciated by all.

The Nordiques were still the local favourites. Each player received an enormous roar from the friendly crowd, though none, it seemed, got as loud a reception as Travis. But then, none of them had been through what Travis had been through this week.

The introductions done, the players began to head for the bench, the starting line-ups remaining on the ice to wait for the anthem. Travis was nervous, but ready. He had hit the crossbar twice in the warm-up. He had felt the warmth of the crowd. He wanted the puck to drop.

A man in a blue blazer was moving towards centre ice. He was carrying a microphone. He spoke first in French, then in English, about a special guest and a special presentation that was going to take place before the anthem.

The crowd was already rising for a better view. Some had recognized who it was that had just moved towards the entrance to the ice surface. The crowd was mumbling, the noise growing, and some fans were pointing and cheering.

Was it Guy Lafleur? Travis wondered. Obviously the crowd recognized whomever it was. It *had* to be a hockey star.

The man in the blue blazer was still introducing the special guest: "*He has come here following*

*last night's game in Montreal to show his continuing
support for Canadian minor hockey . . ."*

It couldn't be Lafleur. It had to be a current
NHL star!

The crowd was all up now, the cheering rising
to a roar as loud as the one that greeted Travis. A
handsome, dark-haired young man in a suit was
moving through the crowd of tournament
officials and about to step onto the ice.

*". . . captain of the Mighty Ducks of Anaheim . . .
Paul Kariya!"*

Despite the roar, Travis heard a voice beside
him.

"I'm dead meat!"

Travis turned and looked at Nish. His friend
had turned the colour of the fresh-flooded ice.
Nish closed his eyes as if he wished he could
make the great Paul Kariya vanish.

The Mighty Ducks' captain was about to find
out that according to some kid's hockey card he
had a long-lost "cousin."

A man was coming out onto the ice behind
Paul Kariya. He was carrying something over his
right arm. It looked like a hockey sweater, with
the same colours as were worn by the Screech
Owls. Paul Kariya took the sweater, and the man
in the blue blazer began talking again in French
and English, switching back and forth between
the two languages. With the noise of the crowd

and the echoes of the Colisée, Travis caught only pieces of what he was saying.

". . . *les sept buts de Guy Lafleur . . . a record that has stood for nearly four decades . . . un effort incroyable . . . so it is with great pleasure that the organizing committee of the fortieth Quebec International Peewee Tournament honours Sarah Cuthbertson!*"

Once more the Colisée burst into a tremendous roar. How, Travis wondered, could the fans keep it up? A stunned Sarah skated towards centre ice, where Paul Kariya congratulated her and then held up the hockey sweater.

It was Sarah's "stolen" sweater! Number 9, with seven velvet pucks sewn on the front – *just like Guy Lafleur's!*

The Colisée crowd seemed to blow like a volcano when they saw it. Some of the Owls on the ice dropped their sticks and gloves and held their hands over their ears, but even their hands and helmets could not keep out the roar.

With Paul Kariya's help, Sarah pulled off the replacement sweater and pulled on the new one. Photographers skidded along the ice to capture the moment, and then Sarah and Paul Kariya, both of them smiling, posed for a picture together while the crowd continued to cheer.

From just behind Travis came Nish's voice again.

"*She'd better not tell him about my card!*"

16

THE MOMENT THE PUCK LEFT THE REFEREE'S hand, Travis knew he had never been in a hockey game quite like this one. It was as if an electrical cord ran from every player and had been connected to the same charge. There was the proud history of the tournament. There was the great size of the rink. There were the peewee ghosts of Guy Lafleur, Wayne Gretzky, Mario Lemieux, Patrick Roy. There was Paul Kariya, the NHL's newest star, watching from the stands. There were television cameras. There were the more than ten thousand fans, the noise like an explosion every time something happened on the ice. And there were the Beauport Nordiques, the crowd favourites, up against the Screech Owls for the divisional championship trophy.

The crowd no longer intimidated Travis. He seemed to take energy from the roar. He still tingled with the surprise of his greeting, still thrilled at the memory of tilting his stick in salute. And he had hit the crossbar during the warm-up.

Sarah seemed inspired by her seven velvet pucks. She played as if possessed by the spirit of

Lafleur. She was all over the ice, checking, attacking, never out of position, never selfish with the puck. Twice she fed Dmitri with breakaway passes, only to have the marvellous Beauport goaltender turn Dmitri away. Once she fed the puck to Travis, coming in fast on left wing, and he ripped a shot that just hit the wrong side of the crossbar. Had it struck the underside, the Owls would be leading. But it struck the top and flew into the crowd, a throng of excited kids scrambling for the souvenir.

But the story today was Nish. Travis had no idea what it was – Paul Kariya's presence, envy over Sarah's velvet pucks, the chance to win the Quebec Peewee – but whatever it was, it was bringing out the best in Nish's game.

Twice in the first period alone, Nish saved goals on plays that already had Jeremy beaten. Once he fell, sliding, and swept away a puck one of the Beauport forwards was about to slip into the open side of the Owls' net. Once he went down on his knees behind Jeremy, who was out of the play, and took a hard, point-blank shot from a Beauport defender straight in the chest, then batted the rebound away with a baseball swing of his stick before the puck could land back in the Owls' crease.

On the ice, Travis had no time to think. The game was so fast, so unpredictable, the action end-to-end and furious. The crowd roared with each rush, cheered each good defensive play. Travis felt wonderful, as if he were part of a huge, well-oiled machine that was demonstrating hockey as it should be played. He was honoured to be part of this game, pleased that he could be out there with these wonderful peewee players and fit right in. Not only that, he was *captain* of one of the teams.

On the bench, Travis could watch – and think. He was inspired by how hard the other Owls were working: Andy all over the ice, little Simon leading rush after rush, Jeremy Weathers leaping to cover rebounds, Jesse Highboy throwing himself in front of shots, Lars ragging the puck until he could see his pass, Data always back, always dependable.

The Nordiques scored first again. Travis was on the ice, and a pass from Nish came too high along the boards for him to handle. The Nordiques' defenceman cradled the puck in his skates, kicked it up to his stick, and sent it fast across the ice to the far winger, waiting just to the side of the goal. Jeremy stopped the one-timer, but Beauport's big centre swiped the rebound out of the air and sent it high into the net.

"My fault," Travis said as he skated back to the bench.

"No," said Nish. "Mine. Bad pass."

The next shift out, Nish made up for it. He intercepted a Beauport pass just beyond centre and stepped around his check before rapping a hard pass off the boards that Dmitri took in full flight.

Dmitri led his defenceman off into the corner and used the boards to drop the puck back to Sarah. He knew she'd be coming in behind. She picked up the puck, moved toward the slot, and hit Travis perfectly on the tape as he broke for the net. He shot as soon as he felt the weight of the puck. The puck flew high – too high, Travis thought at first – and then clicked in off the underside of the crossbar.

Owls 1, Nordiques 1.

"*Un bon but*. Good goal," the winger opposite said as they lined up for the face-off at centre.

Travis looked up. It was the same winger who'd dumped him last game, the one who'd sarcastically said, "*Je t'aime*." But this time there was no sarcasm.

"Thanks," Travis said. Then, as an afterthought: "*Merci*."

The game remained tied 1–1 until there were only ten minutes to go. The crowd was still screaming. The game remained as fast-paced and intense as it had been on that first shift.

Nish again made the key play when he executed a give-and-go with Sarah coming out of the Owls' end. He stickhandled behind his own net, then hit Sarah as she came back over the blueline and cut to the right. The moment Nish passed, he took off, heading straight up ice, and Sarah returned the puck to him on her backhand, the play catching the Beauport forwards by surprise.

Nish put his head down, his skates sizzling even on the chewed-up ice. Travis dug in hard, double-stepping on his right skate before completing his turn and pushing hard on his left skate, his leg fully extended and a flick of his ankle giving him one final surge along the ice.

Nish looked up and saw him. He shifted slightly to pass, Travis hurrying to get a step on the defenceman, who was reading the play. Travis had just enough on him to be free.

Nish tossed the puck ahead of Travis, who was able to scoop it off the boards in full flight.

The defenceman had turned and was giving chase. Travis thought he had the angle, but didn't quite. The defenceman was on him by the blue-line, and even with him as he crossed.

He had only the back pass left! Travis knew what Muck had told him. He knew what had happened last game. *But there was no other play!*

He knew Nish. Travis knew he would still be coming hard. He could hear Nish's stick pounding the ice: the signal that he wanted the puck.

Travis just had time to slip the puck onto his backhand. The defenceman was on him, reaching, ready to bowl him over if necessary. Travis waited, waited, and just as the defenceman completely committed to checking him, he dumped the pass blind behind his back. He spun round as he and the defenceman fell.

Nish had the puck! It had hit his stick perfectly. Travis couldn't have sent a better pass if he had drawn it with a pencil and ruler.

Nish was in, the last Beauport defender racing to cover him. He waited, then did the spinnerama move he usually only dared in practice, spinning right around with his back to the defenceman and carrying the puck past.

The defenceman turned, catching Nish just as he tossed the puck off to Dmitri, who was in all alone.

The crowd roared, and like a thousand jack-in-the-boxes they sprang up in their seats.

Dmitri faked once and drilled a hard shot for the high far side.

Travis was already moving his stick into the air to cheer when the Beauport goalie's blocker flashed high and knocked the puck away.

Nish, still barrelling in past the last defender, picked up the rebound. He turned, moving the puck to his backhand, and was actually skating backwards as he reached around the falling goalie and slipped the puck, barely, into the far side.

Owls 2, Nordiques 1.

Nish hit the boards and crumpled – not hurt, but very happy. He lay there grinning and pumping his fists, waiting for the pile-on.

"*A great goal!*" Travis shouted. "*A video high-lighter!*"

"*You did it, Nish!*" shouted Dmitri. "*You did it!*"

Nish had done it – but there were still ten minutes left.

"*No more fancy stuff!*" Muck shouted, as he sent them back out for the face-off.

Travis felt he was speaking directly to him. No more behind-the-back passes, that was for sure. But it *had* worked!

Muck wanted defensive hockey, and that is what he got. With Sarah killing time by hanging on to the puck and circling ever backwards, the Owls waited until the frustrated Nordiques charged and then dumped – trying at least to cross centre ice first so they wouldn't cause an icing.

When the Beauport team charged, Nish was there. Diving, sliding, and throwing himself across the ice, he broke up play after play, until after one whistle he lay on the ice, completely exhausted. It was the strangest thing Travis had ever seen in a hockey rink. Nish lay there, gasping, and some of the fans began clapping.

The applause rose until everyone in the rink was clapping. Then, as Nish picked himself up off the ice, they rose, and delivered the most incredible standing ovation Travis had ever seen. Even under his helmet, he could feel the hair on the back of his head standing up.

As Nish made his way to the bench, his head hanging down, his stick dragging, the Beauport team decided to pull its goaltender for the extra attacker.

Muck called the one time-out he was allowed, and the Owls skated over to hear what he had to say. But Muck said nothing; he stood behind the bench, Mr. Dillinger at his shoulder, and stared at Nish, gasping on the end of the bench, waiting for him to catch his breath.

Finally, with the referee signalling the end to the time-out, Nish looked up and caught Muck's eye.

"Can you go?" Muck asked.

Nish couldn't even speak. He nodded once and jumped the boards, the rink again exploding into cheers.

What fantastic hockey fans, Travis thought. When Muck said they knew their hockey better than any fans in the world, he wasn't kidding. They came wanting Beauport to win, but they knew that they had seen the most extraordinary effort imaginable from both teams, particularly the heavyset, red-faced defenceman for the Owls, and they were bound to give the Screech Owls and Nish their due.

With their extra attacker, the Nordiques charged relentlessly. Even with Sarah out for the entire final shift, the Owls couldn't gain control of the puck. They couldn't score on the empty net. They couldn't even get an icing.

If it hadn't been for Nish, all would have been lost.

He dived head first to knock a sure goal away from the big Beauport centre. He threw himself into the net three times to block scramble shots that Jeremy couldn't hold. He took the puck off the big centre and faked a rush outside, sending the Nordiques players over the blueline, then circling back into his own end and, with the centre giving chase, heading as fast towards his own goal as he might have rushed the Nordiques' net.

Nish whipped around the net, the big centre right behind him, and dropped the puck onto the backhand so it hit the boards and bounced out again, nestling against the back of the net.

Nish turned instantly and grabbed the puck he had left behind as the big Beauport centre flew out of the play. He stickhandled patiently, then lifted the puck high towards the clock. It slapped back down on the ice just as the horn sounded to end the greatest championship game the Owls had ever played.

They had won the Quebec Peewee!

17

TRAVIS LINDSAY THOUGHT HE KNEW WHAT A great roar was. But he had no idea. What he had heard during his introduction, what he had heard during the presentation of Sarah's sweater, was nothing compared to the roar that went up when they announced the Most Valuable Player for the C division of the Quebec International Peewee Tournament.

". . . WAYNE NISHHHHHHI-KAAWWAAAAAA!"

Players on both sides began banging their sticks on the ice in tribute. The fans, every single one of them, were already on their feet, cheering, screaming, yelling. The noise was deafening.

"*Oh no!*" Nish said, as he spun in a frantic circle beside Travis.

"*What?*" Travis asked.

Then he saw.

The MVP award was to be presented by Paul Kariya. The NHL star had a large silver trophy in his arms, and he was smiling in Nish's direction.

"*I can't go!*" Nish said.

"*Get over there!*" Travis shouted, hoping he could be heard above the cheering.

Reluctantly, red-faced, Nish laid his stick down at his feet and then his gloves. He took off his helmet, the cheers rising, and handed it to Travis, then skated slowly over to where Paul Kariya was waiting with the trophy.

Nish was beet-red by the time he got there.

Paul Kariya reached out, shook his hand, and gave him the trophy. Then he grabbed Nish and hugged him, the crowd erupting with an even greater cheer.

Travis could see Paul Kariya whispering something in Nish's ear. Perhaps he was shouting. He would have to shout to be heard above this.

Nish came back, redder still, but smiling. He raised the MVP trophy as a tribute to the crowd, then to the Beauport team, which made the cheering fans go wild.

"What'd he say to you?" Travis said as Nish gathered his gloves back up.

"Who?" Nish asked.

Travis couldn't believe it. "*Paul Kariya! What did he say?*"

"Oh, that," Nish said nonchalantly. "Just, 'Nice game, cousin.' That's all."

Travis looked at him in shock. Nish was grinning from ear to ear, both arms around his trophy.

They had brought the championship trophy out on the ice. A swarm of officials had gathered, and the man in the blue blazer with the microphone was moving towards the shining silver cup.

Travis could hear his name being called. He could hear the crowd cheering him as he skated.

But he wasn't thinking at all about being captain, or about the cheers. He wasn't even thinking about how, so many years ago, "Terrible Ted" Lindsay of the Detroit Red Wings had hoisted the Stanley Cup high above his head and thus established a grand tradition for victorious team captains ever since.

Travis would do all that. And he would then hand it off to, first, Sarah, and then Nish. He knew he would be bringing Monsieur and Madame Dupont, his billets, out on the ice so they could hold it too. He knew that he would ask for a photograph of him and Nicole with it, something to have that would forever remind him of this wonderful, miraculous moment.

But before any of that he had something else to do. He tried to clear his mind and think only of what Sarah and Nicole had taught him since that moment they dragged him off to "school."

He had shaken the officials' hands. He had the championship trophy in his arms. But now he reached for the microphone.

The man in the blue blazer seemed a little surprised, but he smiled and handed it over.

Travis cleared his throat. He knew the roaring

was dying down, the cheers were stopping. They were quieting down to hear what he had to say.

His hand was shaking as he brought the microphone up to his face.

"*Merci beaucoup, mes amis,*" he began.

"*C'est pour moi et les autres Screech Owls le plus grand honneur des nos vies de hockey . . .*"

He continued without hesitation, his mind remembering perfectly the words and pronunciations that Nicole and Sarah had drilled into him.

He thanked the fans.

He thanked "*le magnifique*" team standing opposite, the Beauport Nordiques.

He thanked the Quebec Peewee Tournament organizers.

He thanked the City of Quebec.

He could have gone on. But no one – not any of the players on the ice, not Muck or any of the coaches, not one of the ten thousand fans – would have heard a word Travis Lindsay was saying over the enormous roar that went up.

The loudest roar of a most extraordinary day.

THE END

The Screech Owls' Home Loss

When a phone call from his best friend, Nish, gets Travis out of bed one bright winter's morning, it looks as if it's going to be the best weekend ever.

The Screech Owls' home town of Tamarack lies beneath a thick fall of snow, topped with a layer of hard, smooth, beautiful ice. The best way to get around town is to strap on a pair of skates and glide – up and down the streets, across lawns and playgrounds, and over farmers' fields. The whole world has become one gigantic skating rink. If only there were a way, thinks Travis, for these two wonderful days to last forever.

But before the weekend is over, Travis wishes it had never begun. One of the Screech Owls lies in a hospital bed, unable to move – the victim of a cowardly drunk driver who has fled the scene of his crime.

Now the Screech Owls must face a challenge that would make the toughest hockey game seem easy. Somewhere in the town of Tamarack a criminal is in hiding, and somehow – for the sake of their friend – Travis and the Screech Owls must find a way to pull together as a team and bring the culprit to justice.

THE SCREECH OWLS SERIES

1. Mystery at Lake Placid
2. The Night They Stole the Stanley Cup
3. The Screech Owls' Northern Adventure
4. Murder at Hockey Camp
5. Kidnapped in Sweden
6. Terror in Florida
7. The Quebec City Crisis
8. The Screech Owls' Home Loss
9. Nightmare in Nagano
10. Danger in Dinosaur Valley
11. The Ghost of the Stanley Cup